THE BLYTHE GIRLS
Helen, Margy, and Rose

THE BLYTHE GIRLS

Helen, Margy, and Rose

or

FACING THE GREAT WORLD

By

LAURA LEE HOPE

Author of "The Blythe Girls: Helen's Strange
Boarder," "The Outdoor Girls of Deepdale,"
"The Bobbsey Twins Camping Out," Etc.

WHITMAN PUBLISHING CO.
RACINE, WISCONSIN

CONTENTS

CONTENTS

The Blythe Girls:
Helen, Margy and Rose

CHAPTER I

Uprooted

"Well, here we are!"

Rose Blythe, fair-haired, blue-eyed and pretty, sat down upon one of the several upturned trunks and looked about her disconsolately.

The apartment was littered with luggage and personal belongings for as far as she could see down the vista of hall that ended abruptly and unpleasantly in a small and dingy dining room.

Everywhere was disorder and confusion, the inevitable result of a hasty moving.

The moving men had been in a tremendous hurry, she thought, resentfully. They might at least have waited to put some of the things in order! This reflection proved, beyond a doubt, two things—that Rose was just turned sixteen and that she had never before experienced the unpleasant business of moving.

"Well, here we are," she repeated gloomily, and her sister Margy, who had been superin-

1

tending the placing of a bundle of umbrellas on top of the swathed and utterly disguised piano, turned to her younger sister with a sympathetic smile.

"Cheer up, child!" she said, in the cheery tone that seemed always to be hiding a laugh. "It really isn't as bad as you look. Just wait till we get things straightened out a bit. You won't know the place."

Margy Blythe was only a year and a half older than Rose, but she seemed more than that. Perhaps it was her dark hair that made the difference. Or perhaps it was only the fact that she was, by nature, practical and clear-thinking, acting often as a check upon her more temperamental sister.

Helen, the third and oldest of the Blythe girls, came in from a last conference with the moving men.

"They are gone," she announced, sinking down upon an immense old couch that seemed far too large for the tiny living room. "And most of our money has gone with them, too. I—I never knew moving was so expensive!"

"Well, if we have enough left to buy us an evening meal, you had better stand and deliver at once, my dear," said Margy, reaching energetically for her hat.

But Rose had crushed her own small straw upon her golden curls and had already possessed herself of the "family pocketbook."

"I'll go, Margy," she announced, glad enough to be away from the disheartening confusion for a little while. You stay with Helen and rest awhile."

"Oh, yes, we'll rest!" said Margy ironically, while Helen called anxiously after the youngest.

"Don't bring in pickled pig's feet and potato salad, the way you did last time, kiddie. We want something filling you know."

"Sure! Roast pork, baked apples, potatoes, green peas and peach pie," returned the youngest, irrepressibly. "As a little provider, I'll tell you right now, I'm there. Whew—now, who may you be?"

This last remark was addressed to a young man who stood in the doorway of the apartment, dangling a curious-looking object in his hand. Upon closer inspection, Rose recognized the young man as the "boss" of the moving men—officially known as the office manager of the Reynolds Moving Company—and the curious-looking object in his hand as a vegetable strainer, grown old in the service of the Blythe family.

"Is this for me?" asked Rose, and at her impish grin the young man grinned back.

"Men overlooked it," he said, adding, with a widening of his grin: "Had a notion you might be needing it soon." And before Rose could properly thank him he had dodged about and was gone.

"Seems to be of a bashful disposition," Rose confided to her two sisters. "But good-looking. I'll say he's the—"

"Rose Blythe, if you use any more of that horrible slang, I'll ship you right back to Riverdale," Helen threatened, and Rose made a laughing face at her.

"If you think that's a threat, you are mistaken, old dear," she gibed. "It's a promise!" With this she fox-trotted across the threshold, went out into the hall, blithely slamming the door to behind her. The girls heard her running lightly down the stairs. There was no elevator in the apartment house in which they had sought shelter, and it was a long, long way to the street.

The two girls left alone in the tumbled apartment looked at each other significantly, and Helen sighed.

"Rose is a dreadful problem," she said. "It seems only yesterday that she was a kiddie, and now—look at her!"

"Pretty easy to look at, I should say," retorted Margy briskly, and Helen took her up with unusual vehemence.

"That's just the point!" she cried. "If Rose were an ugly duckling I shouldn't worry. But she is so pretty, and now that we are here in New York—" She left the sentence unfinished and Margy looked at her quizzically.

"Adrift in a big city, is that it?" she asked, and Helen laughed.

"Not exactly adrift as long as we have this apartment to anchor to," she said. Then she gave a glance of discouragement at the confusion around her. "But isn't it an awful place?" she asked.

"Well, we won't make it any better by sitting and looking at it," suggested Margy practically.

"Anyway, the view from the windows isn't so bad."

Margy crossed over to one of the large windows in the living room and her sister followed, putting an arm about her shoulders. What they saw was, as Margy had said, "not so bad." The apartment house in which they had taken refuge was situated on a rather steep rise of ground and before it was a gently sloping vista of open lots and scattered apartment houses. In a short time all these vacant lots would be occupied no doubt, by ugly, sky-towering buildings, but for the present the view, such as it was, was not greatly obstructed.

"Feel that breeze," said Helen, as a faint puff of air blew the fair hair about her face.

"And listen to that hurdy-gurdy," retorted her sister disgustedly, as she leaned further out of the window to get a better view of the wilted-looking musician and his decrepit hand organ. Several children had gathered around and were listening in apparent enjoyment to the tinny strains of the sextette from Lucia, played in modern jazz tempo. "Anyway, the kiddies are happy," added Margy.

Helen sighed involuntarily as she turned from the window.

"I suppose we had better unpack the dishes first," she said. "If Rose ever gets back with her pork and her peach pie we'll probably need them."

Helen Blythe was a tall, slender girl with a mass of ash-blonde hair which she wore piled high on her head. She was a great deal like Rose, though not so vivid a type. Whereas her hair was fair, it was very light, almost washed out, while Rose's bobbed curls were a warm gold, seeming, in some lights, almost red. Although her eyes, like the eyes of her younger sister, were blue, Helen's were dreamy and brooding while those of the younger girl sparkled with life and vivacity.

Helen was the artist of the family. In Riverdale, a small town on Long Island where they had lived for many years, she had been pronounced unusually talented and a great future had been predicted for her by admiring neighbors and friends.

But Helen, though she loved their praise, was far too level-headed to be spoiled by it. She knew that she had a certain amount of talent and that she loved to paint and draw, but she knew also that it would require years of patient study and effort before she could hope to accomplish anything great.

They had been a happy family in the big, rambling old homestead with its many rooms and air of comfort. Then their mother had died, three years before.

Helen was very like her mother, who had cherished dreams of an artistic career and had died with those dreams still unfulfilled. Helen knew, as she thought fondly and longingly of that tall, placid, dreamy-eyed mother, that her art had, after all, found the highest form of expression. She had filled the home with beauty and sunshine and harmony of thought, made it so attractive, so bright and pleasant to them all that they could not bear to leave it and always went back to it eagerly as the one spot of perfect peace and harmony.

Yet her mother had whispered to her in that last hour when all things seemed to stand still in a breathless, frightened silence and as the heart of the home prepared to take the sunshine with her, had whispered so faintly that Helen could scarcely make out the import of the words.

"Make the most of your talent, dear. Don't let any one discourage you or turn you aside from your purpose. If you could do—what your mother has always dreamed of doing—I think I should be—very happy—in Heaven—"

Helen had cried from the depths of a breaking heart:

"Mother darling, I will try, oh, I will try!"

Then the sunshine had gone, and the dear home was a home no longer, but just a place in which to live.

Her father, once so care-free, rollicking and merry, could not long survive that departure. It was as though a plant, thriving in the light of the sun, had been suddenly transplanted to a dark cellar.

Just a year after their mother's death the Blythe girls had faced each other in the living room of the old house and knew themselves not only motherless and fatherless, but almost penniless.

Their father, though a brilliant man and lovable, had never been a financial success. He had made enough for them to live on comfortably, and that he deemed sufficient.

He had left a small life insurance, and it was on this that the girls had lived for two of the most miserable years they had known.

They had not owned the old homestead. If they had, their problem would have been fairly simple. With the income from the life insurance and what money they could have made by taking small positions in Riverdale, they might have managed to get along comfortably enough.

But the home was rented and the rental seemed alarmingly high to the girls. It had

been so large, in fact, that they had not been
able to live on the income from their small in-
vested capital and had been forced to see the
principal gradually dwindle.

Margy, the practical one, had long since
urged that they give up the house—which was a
"white elephant eating its head off"—pack up
"a few sticks of furniture," and move to the
city where they could find employment and have
a chance of making enough money to live on.

Helen, because of her mother, had dreaded
giving up the old house, but at last had been
forced to see the wisdom of Margy's viewpoint.

So they had taken stock of their assets, which
were few, and their liabilities, which were many,
and had found that, after scrupulously paying
all they owed, they had enough to pay the moving men and the first month's rental on a New
York apartment. With economy they might
be able to meet expenses, feed and clothe themselves for another month. That was all. They
did not dare to think beyond that time.

"Oh, nonsense," Margy had said, in her most
optimistic mood. "By the end of a month we
shall have scrumptious jobs and just be rolling in money!"

CHAPTER II

PROBLEMS

THE great step had now been taken, the moving was over, and the Blythe girls were fairly set for the great adventure.

After much searching and skinning of knuckles, Margy and Helen succeeded in discovering the hiding place of the barrel of dishes and Margy, seemingly miraculously, drew forth a hammer and tack-puller from one of the boxes.

"What do you bet they are all broken?" said the latter, cheerfully. "I mean the dishes, not my knuckles—though there is an even chance either way," she added ruefully.

"You poor dear. Let me take a hand now. There—and you always said I never had any strength!"

The cover was off, and the dishes that had been packed with such loving care were disclosed. Most of the china had been decorated by their mother and was priceless to them in consequence.

Not a piece was broken, which seemed to them an omen of good luck.

10

Carefully they transported it to the little cubby-hole of a kitchen behind the dark and dingy dining room.

They resolutely kept up a cheerful front while Margy hastily scrubbed down the shelves of an inconvenient cupboard and Helen washed and wiped the precious china till it gleamed.

When the shelves of the closet were freshly lined with white paper and the dishes safely bestowed upon them, the girls felt somehow better and more cheerful.

"We have something that looks a little bit more like home, anyway," said Margy.

"Now for the table linen. Have you any idea where it was packed, Nell?"

Helen admitted that she had not the slightest idea, and together they went in search of it.

They found it presently and proceeded to set the table. When it was all done they sat down for a moment to take breath and looked at each other.

"The kiddie isn't back yet," said Helen, voicing the thought of them both. "Now where do you suppose she can be?"

A door slammed noisily at the end of the hall and Rose herself answered the question.

She came into the kitchen, flushed and bright-eyed, to meet a reproach from Helen.

"You must try not to slam doors like that, Rose," she said. "We are not in a house all

by ourselves now, you know, and the other ten-
ants might object if we made too much noise.''

"Sort of like being in jail, isn't it?" queried
Rose, with a grin that tried to be cheerful but
deceived no one. "All right, I'll try to remember, Nell. Now look here and see what I
brought you. Isn't this ever so much better
than stodgy old roast pork?"

She undid the parcel in her hands and proudly displayed its contents.

The girls watched with dismay as she ex-
tracted three large pickles, some indigestible
looking celery salad, a chunk of highly-
seasoned meat loaf, and some of the greasiest
doughnuts it had ever been their bad fortune to look upon.

Even Margy was disgusted this time and
slapped on a hat over her disordered hair, to
go out and get some "regular food."

"Well, of all the old fogies!" exclaimed Rose,
as the door closed after her disgruntled sister.
"What's the matter with this dinner, I'd like
to know? It's good and nourishing, isn't it?"

"Yes, and indigestible," said Helen wearily.
"I do wish you would use a little more judg-
ment, kiddie."

"And I do wish you would stop calling me
'kiddie!'" said Rose, suddenly vehement. "It
sounds so silly, especially, since I'm almost
grown up."

A few minutes later Margy arrived with

some lamb chops and peas, and it was not long before a pleasant aroma was wafting its fragrance through the dingy and disorderly rooms.

They ate, too, oh, how they ate! with the ravenous appetites of young folks who have gone without sustenance for an unusually long period. After they had eaten they cleared up the dishes with a little more enthusiasm and set to work getting the beds ready for the night.

This was not such an easy task, since both the big double bed and the cot which was to accommodate Rose were leaning against the wall in the living room with a small army of bundles and boxes piled against them.

When the big bed had finally been set up in the larger of the two cubby-holes that must answer for bedrooms, the mattress unearthed and dragged to its proper resting place upon the springs, the bedding found and sorted, the girls were about ready to drop with fatigue.

"And still we have that old cot to move," cried Rose, as she flung herself upon the bed, kicked off one shoe and rubbed a painful instep. "To tell the truth, I'd rather hang up on a peg all night than budge again."

"Poor kiddie," said Helen, looking pityingly at the bundle of discontent curled up on the foot of the bed. "You don't have to budge. Just get in your nightie and we'll have the cot ready in a jiffy."

"You are just spoiling that girl, Nell," said

Margy, in a low tone, as she and Helen went back for the cot. "You shouldn't wait on her like that. She could be getting out the bed linen. We none of us feel as fresh as the morning, you know."

At last everything was in readiness. The doors and windows were all locked, the lights all out and nothing remained but to cuddle into bed and—sleep.

But they did not sleep. Over-fatigue, the strangeness of their surroundings, anxiety about their future, all combined to keep them wakeful and restless during the greater part of the night.

It was hot, too, breathlessly hot and stuffy, in their little cubby-holes where the only air that entered their windows was through an open court.

Somebody in the apartment below them was having a late party, playing jazz upon a player piano whose syncopated rhythm jarred unbearably upon their taut nerves.

It was horrible, a nightmare of sights and sounds and smells that assailed their senses and made them long achingly for the rambling old homestead in Riverdale where there was nothing to break the stillness but the song of crickets and the croaking of the frogs in the pool behind the house, where a soft, flower-scented breeze made bearable even the hottest nights.

It was nearly dawn before any of them fell asleep, and the sun was high in the heavens before they opened heavy eyes upon the problems of a new day.

"Isn't the noise awful?" asked Margy, as she sat upon the edge of the bed, swinging a listless foot. "I feel as though I had to shout to make you hear at all."

Helen brushed her hair thoughtfully and nodded.

"It wouldn't be so bad if we were not on a street car line—"

"And in that case we should have had to pay just twice as much for this flat as we are doing," said Margy. Then she added, with a humorous twist of her mouth: "And if you can tell me how on earth that could be managed, I'll be very proud of you, Helen Blythe."

"And I," said Helen, with a wry smile at her reflection in the mirror, "would be very proud of myself!"

CHAPTER III

The Strainer Man

AFTER breakfast, which consisted of scrambled eggs, burned toast and not very excellent coffee, Helen called a council in the living room.

"We have to decide what we are going to do, girls, and then do it as quickly as possible."

"It seems to me it will be a great deal easier to decide what we are going to do than to do it," said Rose, sitting cross-legged on the couch and munching at one of the very greasy doughnuts she had brought home the night before. "If all you read in the paper is true, there are a great many more girls wanting jobs than there are jobs to go round."

"If you begin your career by believing all the papers say, I certainly feel sorry for you," remarked Margy roundly. Then she said, as her eyes fell upon the partially devoured doughnut: "I wish you would put down that horrible thing, Rose. It makes me sick just to look at it."

"I am putting it down, the right way," chuckled Rose. "And as long as it only makes me

16

sick, you should worry. But go on, Nell. You were saying something, weren't you?"

"I thought I was," retorted Helen dryly. "And I think you had better not take this matter so lightly, Rose. It really isn't anything to laugh about."

"Well, you don't see me laughing do you?" protested Rose, her mouth full of doughnut. "To tell you the truth, I am just about ready to burst into tears only that I know it would ruin my complexion."

"Not half as much as that doughnut will," laughed Margy, adding seriously as she turned back to Helen: "You are right about our deciding at once what we are going to do, Nell. You will stay at home here of course," she added decidedly, "and keep house for us and go on with your art. As for me," she hesitated, doubtfully, "I can use the typewriter and I know a little about stenography—"

"Oh, you're in luck Margy Blythe!" cried Rose, abandoning her cross-legged position on the couch and speaking eagerly. Stenogs draw down tremendous salaries, and with your brains and looks and everything it won't be any time at all before you get to be a private secretary. Then your boss—he's sure to be a millionaire—will fall in love with you—"

"I suppose he won't have anything else to do," agreed Margy, dryly adding, with a chuckle: "You forget, Rose, that it is only in

story books that the employer is young and
handsome. Probably my boss, if I am lucky
enough to get one, will be a crabbed old body,
blind in one eye and with chronic indigestion.''

''What difference would that make,'' said
Rose calmly, ''if he had plenty of money?''

Helen and Margy looked at their little sister
in wide-eyed surprise and were about to launch
on a lecture when they saw that she was laughing.

''Well, now that I am successfully married
off to my wealthy employer,'' said Margy, turning with a laugh to the still serious Helen,
''what shall we do with this little imp here?
She really isn't good for anything—except to
be spanked.''

''What do you want to do, Rose?'' asked
Helen.

''I'm going to get a store job. They pay
pretty good money and you get good experience
if you are willing to start from the bottom and
work up.'' Rose spoke defiantly as if expecting
opposition and was ready for it. ''And it's
lots of fun, too. You meet so many people and
—everything,'' she ended, rather lamely.

The two older girls did not react to this plan
as she had feared they would. They merely
exchanged significant glances and then looked
long and thoughtfully at Rose.

''Oh, stop staring—do!'' the latter exclaimed
vehemently, fretted by this prolonged scrutiny.

"Really, I'm not a curiosity—only an ordinary girl trying to find the best and quickest way of making money."

"You could study stenography too—go to school with me," Margy began slowly, but Rose shook her golden bobbed head emphatically.

"I don't want to go to school. I had enough of it in Riverdale. What I want to do now is to make some real money—and see something of life."

"Oh, you will do that all right," said Margy dryly. "There is one thing about a job in a department store. You certainly do meet people of all kinds."

Helen gave Margy a warning glance and put an arm about her youngest sister.

"It's all right, dear, if you are sure that is what you want to do," she said with an explosive sigh of relief as Rose snuggled closer. "If at any time you want to change, to do something else, we can arrange that, too. Of course, the most important thing just now is to start the money rolling in."

Rose jumped to her feet, her eyes shining.

"You are a perfect brick, Nell. I thought maybe you wouldn't let me. Oh, dear! where is my hat?"

"Where are you going now?" asked Helen, bewildered, as always, by her sister's abrupt changes of mood.

"To get a job, of course," replied the girl.

But, as she charged toward the hall, she was caught and held firmly by the practical Margy.

"Hold your horses, my dear," she drawled. "Do you think jobs grow on trees around here, just waiting to be picked up?"

"Let me go!" cried Rose impatiently, but Helen added her voice to Margy's.

"I'll need you at home to-day, Rose," and Rose knew that, for all Helen's gentleness, when she spoke in that tone she generally meant what she said. "We have to unpack and get to rights and I couldn't possibly do it all by myself."

"And to-night we will get a paper and look up ads," added Margy, releasing her hold of the crestfallen Rose. "You have to go about this business systematically, dear. Now be a good girl and take off your hat."

Rose obeyed, flinging the hat among a clutter of boxes in one corner of the room.

"Oh, well, all right," she said, sulkily. "If I have to stay in this hole—"

"It's no worse for you than for the rest of us!" began Margy heatedly, and Helen hastily assumed her role of peacemaker.

Rose was often irritating and capricious, and Margy possessed a temper that got the better of her at times, so that Helen often found it a hard task to keep the peace between the two.

"We haven't said a word about what I am going to do," she reminded them cheerfully.

"And as I am not at all sure about it myself, I should welcome suggestions."

Rose said nothing. She had gone over to the window and was sulkily staring down at the busy street.

Margy looked at her sister in surprise.

"Why, I thought we had settled all that," she said. "You are to stay at home and keep house for us and go on with your art studies. I should think you would be able to take a course in the afternoons so that you wouldn't have to give up your evenings."

Helen shook her head, and there was an infinite wistfulness in her eyes.

"I should like that, of course," she admitted. "But you know courses cost money—"

"Pshaw! The kiddie and I will soon be making money enough to put you through a dozen courses, you dear old simpleton," cried Margy gayly. Then, as she saw that Helen was not fully convinced, she added: "And maybe you will be able to sell some of your sketches after a while, Nell—"

"Say, girls, who do you suppose is coming?" cried Rose, turning to them, her face all animation again. "It's that good-looking strainer man!"

CHAPTER IV

The First Day

The two sisters exchanged a look of helplessness.

"Now what do you suppose the child means by that?" asked Margy, as Rose made a dash down the long hall toward the kitchen. "The heat must have affected her brain!"

But there came a ring at the doorbell at that moment and Rose pressed the buzzer in the kitchen that magically unlocked the downstairs door. That buzzer was one of the few things about the apartment that Rose liked. It was as fascinating to her as a new toy to a child and she was delighted to be able to use it—especially for the admittance of the "good-looking strainer man."

The latter proved to be none other than Joe Morris, the young man who had so sheepishly presented Rose with the family strainer on the preceding afternoon.

He was looking sheepish again now as he stood twirling his cap in the doorway, and the impish Rose had a moment of wondering whether he had taken the expression off over night or had worn it to bed with him!

It was Helen who had presence of mind enough to invite the young man in and ask him what he wanted.

"I suppose you will think I am taking a great liberty—and probably I am," he said in a pleasant voice that exactly matched his nice face. "But I got to thinking of you three girls here alone without a man to drive a nail for you or help you in any way, and I reckoned maybe you wouldn't think it too bold of me if I offered to set your furniture to rights for you, and maybe hang a picture or two."

"I bet he swings a wicked hammer," murmured Rose in a stage whisper that carried, as it was meant to do. Joe Morris flushed and grinned good-naturedly.

"I'll bet I do," he retorted. Then he turned cajolingly to Helen. "Are you going to let me prove my fitness for the job of all-around handy man?" he asked.

Helen hesitated, feeling greatly embarrassed. It was hard for her to take favors from any one, but they certainly did need a man's strength in the work of getting to rights. And Joe Morris was an extremely likable young fellow whose smile was hard to resist.

"It doesn't seem right to take your time," she objected faintly, but he waved aside this objection as immaterial.

"My time is my own to-day to do with as I will," he proclaimed. "This is my day of rest—"

"And you propose to spend it in the quiet pastime of hanging pictures," said the practical Margy. "You have a funny way of taking your rest, Mr. Morris."

"For goodness' sake, set him to work, Helen. What are you waiting for?" cried Rose. "Here's a man who wants to work. Better snap him up before he changes his mind."

"There speaks the modern business girl," said Joe Morris, turning his laughing gaze upon the youngest Blythe girl.

"Not yet, but soon!" she retorted flippantly, adding, in response to the young fellow's puzzled stare: "I haven't had a chance to look for a job yet."

"Well, you ought to land one in a hurry," said Joe Morris.

The young moving man seemed to be everywhere at once, pulling, hauling, suggesting, and interspersing his labor with jokes that amused the girls and kept from them a full realization of the terrific heat and their own great weariness.

There was satisfaction in the work too, for, as though by magic, the apartment began to take shape and form and color, becoming neat and almost homelike as the familiar furniture found convenient resting places.

At last all was accomplished and Joe Morris suggested refreshments.

Helen, thinking that he meant to invite himself to lunch, was dismayed. There was not a thing in the house to eat except the unpalatable delicatessen fare that Rose had brought them the night before, and she was hastily forming plans for slipping out to market unobserved when the young man solved her problem for her.

"There's a little restaurant on the next block," he said. "Just opened about a week ago, and I hear they have pretty good eats. Let's go and prove it."

Helen demurred, for she felt that they were accepting too much from the agreeable young fellow, but the two other girls overbore her objections and hustled her forth into the burning street.

It was terrible weather, July heat in June, and the city gleamed like a bowl of molten gold beneath the fierce rays of the sun.

The cool interior of the little restaurant to which Joe Morris piloted them was very grateful, and they sank down in the stiff and uncomfortable seats about the small white-topped table with sighs of relief. The place was half full of people seeking like relief from the heat, and as Joe Morris expertly ordered luncheon the girls looked about them with interest.

It was their first real contact with genuine

New Yorkers, and they were disappointed.

The clientele seemed mostly composed of middle-aged women, looking discouraged and bedraggled and wilted by the terrific heat.

But this was not the real New York of romantic fiction, they reminded themselves. Because they were low in funds they had been forced to take an apartment well up toward the Two Hundredths, and that, as Rose had discontentedly remarked, was almost as bad as not living in New York at all.

They delightedly ate the tasty luncheon Joe Morris ordered for them and were reluctant to leave the cool interior of the restaurant for the dinginess and heat of their little five-room flat.

"You girls didn't know when you were well off," Joe Morris told them, as he paid the check and followed them to the sweltering street. "Any one who has a chance to stay in Riverdale, especially in such a delightful old house as you had there, and then comes to this dirty, noisy burg—" He did not finish the sentence, but shook his head as one surprised and dismayed by the idiocy of most mortals.

"As it happens," said Rose with a shake of her golden head, "we didn't have any choice."

Joe Morris regarded her speculatively for a moment while Margy flung her sister a look of reproof at having thus let a comparative stranger into their family secrets.

"That's pretty tough luck," said the young moving man at last, and they finished the short walk to the apartment house in thoughtful silence.

Once at the door of the apartment he had helped to put in order, Joe Morris hesitated. It was evident that he was reluctant to go, but it was equally evident that he had no further excuse for lingering. He had done all he could do and the polite and proper thing for him to do was to say good-bye without further delay.

The bashfulness that had characterized his actions the day before had returned and he found great difficulty in making the simple request that the girls accompany him to a moving picture show that evening.

Helen thanked him but refused, saying that though they were very grateful to him for his kindness they would be too tired to go anywhere that evening.

When he found that nothing could make her change her mind, Morris at last took his departure, saying that he hoped to see them soon again.

CHAPTER V

Good News

Thanks to Joe Morris and their own exertions, dinner that evening was not such a hectic affair as it had been the night before. The heat had marred their appetites, but the food soothed and rested them.

Rose had bought a paper of a passing newsboy, and during the meal had sat with the want advertisement section spread out beside her plate, devouring the sheet as though it were a page from the Arabian Nights.

"There are no ends of places for you, Margy," she said once, looking up to regard her sister enviously over the top of the paper. "All you have to do is just step out and grab a place for a typist, stenog or private secretary."

"Don't I wish it were as simple as all that!" exclaimed Margy ruefully, as she munched on a piece of celery. "I imagine I'll have to do more than just put my hand in the grab bag, kid—er, excuse me—Rose."

Rose looked up suspiciously from her paper, but Margy's expression was grave enough to lull her suspicions to rest. She returned to a perusal of the paper.

"There are plenty of ads for file clerks; but that's one thing I know I haven't any talent for."

"The only one," murmured Margy wickedly, and Helen threw her a warning glance.

But Rose was far too deeply absorbed in her occupation to notice the sarcasm.

"Look! Here it is!" she cried in triumph, running around the table so that Helen might share her joy. "Here is the very position I have been looking for!"

She held a white finger over a particular place in the column, and Helen read an advertisement for a clerk in a department store, "good salary to start and splendid opportunities for advancement."

"I hope you get it, dear, or one like it," said Helen, as she rose to remove the dishes. "We surely do need a wage earner in this family right away!"

But in spite of the need, it seemed for a weary while as though no one of the three Blythe girls was to be permitted to earn any money at all.

They soon learned that, in spite of the glittering promises of the want advertisements, employers of all sorts and kinds invariably demanded one thing of them—experience. And that one thing they did not have.

It hampered them terribly. They began to hate the very word, experience. It seemed that without that elusive thing they were to be denied even a decent living in that great heartless city which their reading had endowed with so much glamor.

"But you have to get your experience somewhere!" Rose had wailed after one particularly discouraging day. "All these experienced people have to start some time. And when they start, they have to start like us—without experience."

"There are a few positions that don't demand experience," Helen reminded her gently. "But you say yourself, you won't even consider them."

"And I won't!" cried Rose passionately, almost in tears. "I could have been an errand girl running around all day for a little bit of money that wouldn't begin to cover expenses."

"But if it gave you experience—" suggested Helen, still more gently, but Rose only shook her head stubbornly.

"I would rather starve," she said, and the older girl knew she meant it.

If only there were money to train the girl for some special occupation or profession, she thought wistfully. But there was not. There was not enough to make it possible for Helen to continue her art lessons.

"How much have we got left, Nell?"

Margy spoke from her corner, where she had pretended to be reading a book, with such suddenness that the two girls started.

Helen hesitated, pretending not to understand Margy's question.

"How much what?" she evaded.

"You know what I mean as well as I do," Margy told her brusquely. "I want to know how much money we have between us and starvation."

Helen's fair skin suddenly became suffused with color. She turned her eyes away from Margy's searching ones.

"We have just enough—to last for another two weeks," she said, in a voice that was almost inaudible.

"Enough to buy us food and pay our expenses traveling back and forth?" Margy continued inexorably, and Helen nodded.

"Then, at the end of the two weeks, what do we do?" Margy's harsh young voice too had sunk till it was almost a whisper. "What do we do then, Nell?"

"Don't ask her! You know as well as she does!" cried Rose, with a protective arm flung suddenly about her eldest sister. "If we don't find something to do before the end of this week, we'll starve, that's all! We'll not be paid in advance, you know," she added bitterly.

"We have to get some money some way," said Margy, as though talking to herself. "Before the end of this week I am going to have a job!''

But she did not—and neither did Rose.

Another week lagged on like a long nightmare while Helen, with an ingenuity born of desperation made each dollar do the work of three.

At last it came to the point one morning when Rose and Margy left the house actually hungry.

Helen, listlessly clearing up after the meal was in even worse shape, for she, when the girls had not noticed, had given them part of her food also, knowing that they, more than she, must be sustained for the day's discouraging round.

She herself had tried to work at her sketches, but was too ridden by fear and worry to accomplish anything worth while.

Joe Morris called occasionally, but the girls were too taken up with their own problems to welcome him very cordially. Then, too, Helen knew that the family budget did not include entertaining. She could not afford to ask Joe Morris to dinner just then, and she was not willing to accept hospitality from him that she could not return.

So, after several of his invitations had been refused, the young man gradually gave up calling. Rose missed him most, but it was not long before she, too, became so absorbed in the fight they were making to think about anything else.

On this particular morning when the girls had gone, half nourished and discouraged, from the house, Helen got out all her old sketches and looked them over carefully.

She took up one which she had appropriately entitled "By the Brook."

It was a pretty little scene, just a woodland grove with some towering trees in the foreground, in the background tangled undergrowth with a brook purling its merry way between moss-grown banks. Pretty—and realistic too. But there were faults. Helen recognized them even while she was at a loss to tell just how they could be remedied.

There was another, just a simple vista of hillside and trees and blowing leaves. One could see the wind in the picture, almost feel the impact of it. The wildly blowing leaves, the scudding clouds across the sky, the half-veiled sun— Yes, it was good, thought Helen, with a quick thrill of pride in her work. She had done something there, portrayed action by means of color, painted her thought upon the blank canvas. With a sigh, half of hope, half of fear, she put it down and picked up another.

Not so good, this one. She had loved doing it, but it had never quite suited her. An old man sat upon a rustic bridge fishing idly in the heat of noonday. One knew it was hot by the intense stillness of the picture. But the old man did not care. He was too engrossed in his favorite sport to think of the heat. Beside him was an old basket, containing several limp witnesses to his skill. Well done enough, that part. But the sky—there was the trouble. The sky had never been quite right. Darken it a trifle? No, that would spoil it.

What if she did not, after all, possess that talent that her mother, her relatives and friends had credited her with? Suppose she was just one of those millions of poor girls deluded by the belief of future greatness, thinking they possessed a gift which had never been theirs!

She put away the sketches drearily. It had been in her mind to take the best of the collection, find out the names and addresses of two or three art dealers from the telephone directory, and try to sell them some of her work.

"But it is no use," she concluded. "They aren't good enough. And, besides, she gave an apprehensive glance at the clock, "it is almost time to get lunch."

Either Margy or Rose was almost sure to drop in around noon for a bite to eat and some encouragement before they began the dreary afternoon round.

Encouragement! thought Helen wistfully. She had not much of that to offer them—and still less of refreshment.

She was examining with clouded brow the pitifully empty pantry when the door opened

and slammed shut and Rose came down the long
hall into the kitchen.

She flung off her hat and sat down in a chair,
drooping wearily.

"No use, Nell," she said. "Nobody wants me.
I think I've tried about every place there is that
amounts to anything and I—I'm just sick and
tired of living. I never thought it would be—
like this! I wonder what luck Margy has
had."

Poor Margy! She could have answered her
sister's question most emphatically several
times that day. "What kind of luck had she
had?" No luck at all—the worst kind of luck—
the—but this is how it happened.

Like Rose, Margy had started out hopefully
enough that morning. As usual, she had
scanned the list of "Help Wanted" and had
selected from it the advertisements that
seemed most promising.

First on the list was the name of Mr. Rosenbaum, Efficiency Expert. This gentleman
seemed badly in need of a stenographer and
something invincibly optimistic in Margy assured her that she was just the person for the
place.

Her optimism received its first shock, however, when she found herself in a bare cubby-
hole of an outer office in company with several
other applicants for the position.

There were girls of all types and classes.

But, whether brunettes or blondes, whether shabbily dressed or garishly dressed, there was an expression common to them all, an expression of expectancy and strain. Every time the door of Mr. Rosenbaum's inner office opened, there was an eager turning of heads, a pathetic preening of feathers as the next in line was admitted to the Presence.

So the line moved slowly up until Margy found herself next the door.

Mr. Rosenbaum must be very particular, she reflected. It seemed to her that some one of the girls who had been admitted to the private office only to come out of it, weary and crestfallen, must have ability enough to fill the position of stenographer to Mr. Rosenbaum, Efficiency Expert.

Perhaps—her heart began to beat wildly at the thought—she was to be the chosen one! If only she could go home to her sisters and tell them that the awful anxiety of the last few days was at an end, that she had secured a position, would on the morrow actually start making money! If only—

A drawling, slightly nasal voice at her elbow broke rudely into the dream.

"From the country, ain't you?" asked the voice, and Margy turned sharply to find the owner of it, a pert, black-eyed, gum-chewing young person.

"I'm from Long Island—which isn't exactly

the backwoods,'' Margy returned rather coldly.
The girl grinned good-naturedly.

"Just as bad,'' she said. "Ought to buy
yourself some new clothes, girlie. Now, if
you'd let me tell you what to get—''

Margy turned from her, her face flaming,
just as the door of the office opened and a lan-
guid office boy appeared. He surveyed the remaining applicants with an indolent eye.

Margy stepped forward, eagerly.

"I'm next,'' she began, but was waved back
by a peremptory gesture of a lean and freckled
hand.

"Job's filled,'' said the youth succinctly.
"You're wasting your time here.''

Half-blinded by chagrin and disappointment,
Margy found her way from the office and from
the building. The pert, black-eyed girl had followed closely after her, evidently with the inten-
tion of imparting more advice upon the subject
of the kind of clothes she thought Margy should
wear.

She was lost in front of the elevators, however, and, with a sigh of relief Margy found
herself at last upon the street and alone. She
felt wilted and very tired, but with a strenuous
effort managed to banish the thought of fatigue
from her mind. The day was just begun and
there were still so many places to go!

She consulted the next address on her list,
and started out again.

Another disappointment—and another—and another— Resolutely Margy continued the weary round while her feet began to feel like balls of fire. It was not until a creeping faintness warned her that she must rest, for a short time, anyway, that she turned into a little restaurant with white-topped tables and a great clatter of dishes. The waitress brought her a plate of rolls and a cup of hot tea. The refreshment, meager as it was, brought fresh courage, and Margy sallied forth again to meet the ordeal of the afternoon.

She suffered rebuff after rebuff until the dreary round became almost automatic. One address after the other, one tall, gaunt office building after another, all exactly alike.

At last there was only one address left, and Margy forced herself toward it. All her self-confidence had deserted her. Her shoes were dusty. She had passed a bootblack and debated with herself whether she would spend a precious dime for a shine, had decided against the extravagance. She had caught a glimpse of herself in a mirror as she had glanced into a shop in passing and had been startled and shocked by her reflection. That was never Margy Blythe, that drawn, haggard, white-faced girl!

Then on again, to the last address in the list. It was the least promising of them all—a clerkship in a lawyer's office. Margy felt sure she

would not get the place, but one could not afford
to overlook a chance.

The office building when she came to it was
an imposing, newly erected, very modern affair,
and Margy, after putting one timid, dust-
stained foot over the grandeur of its threshold,
felt a wild desire to fly from the spot forever.
Instead she went stubbornly on to find herself
in a large foyer with a winding stairway leading into the upper regions and a double set of
elevators on either side of the stairway.

Choosing the stairs as a less conspicuous
means of ascent than the elevator, Margy
mounted to the second floor and found herself
hopelessly confused by an intricate network of
corridors with doors opening in to them.

She was forced at last to consult a pompous
dignitary who patiently explained that she had
misread the directions to the offices of Vail and
Vail, who were really located on the sixteenth
floor. The best thing to do, he told her, with
marked condescension for her ignorance, was
to descend again to the main floor and from
there take an express elevator to the sixteenth
floor.

Margy thanked him and made her weary way
down to the first floor again. She found the
express elevator at last and was whirled up to
the sixteenth floor with a speed that made her
dizzy. Then again began the puzzled hunt

through the network of corridors for the right office.

There it was at last—Vail and Vail, Attorneys, Margy leaned against the wall for a moment to steady the trembling of her lips. Then, summoning her last drop of courage, the girl reached for the door, pushed it open—

"Hey, there, shut that door! Isn't there draft enough without—"

The sharp complaining voice paused as the owner of it surveyed Margy critically. He was a funny, dried-up, little man, with bright black eyes, a hooked nose much too big for his face, and a wide, thin-lipped mouth.

"Well, who are you? Didn't you hear me say to close the door?"

Margy closed the door quickly and stood with her back against it, trembling.

"I saw your advertisement in the paper," she began in a weak voice. "I—I have come to apply for the position if it is not already filled."

"It is," snapped the unpleasant little man, turning his back squarely upon her. "Shut the door quickly after you. I have a dreadful cold."

Out in the corridor again, Margy wondered whether she ought to laugh or cry. The whole thing would have been ludicrous, had it not been so nearly tragic.

What to do now? Where to go? Home?

Confess that she had failed again? Not yet—
not while there was one forlorn little hope left!

For that morning, scanning the "Help
Wanted" column, she had come across a two-
line advertisement. A lady by the name of
Miss Pepper needed a social secretary. Margy
had noted this address with the others, but had
not seriously considered investigating it. Social secretary! The idea of Margy Blythe in
that capacity brought a grim little smile to her
lips. Then she straightened with a swift resolution.

"I won't be a quitter," she told herself. "I'll
go and see this Pepper person if it is the last
thing I do on earth!"

Helen was getting an all too inadequate dinner and Rose was helping her listlessly when
they heard the sound of a key turning in the
lock. The hall door opened and slammed shut.
Even Rose, discouraged as she was, straightened up eagerly at the sound. It was not a de-
feated sound. Somehow it had a note of triumph in it.

Margy's voice came to them before Margy
herself appeared.

"It's all right, girls!" she shouted. "Everything's all right! I've got it!"

CHAPTER VI

Miss Pepper

"Got what?" cried Helen and Rose, as they literally fell upon Margy and dragged her into the kitchen, bombarding her with questions.

"Got a position, you sillies," Margy retorted, half way between laughter and tears. "What did you suppose I meant—the plague or something?"

"You will have something worse than the plague if you don't tell us about it in a hurry," threatened Rose, wildly. "Are you going to tell us what sort of job you've got or have I got to drag it out of you?"

"Stop shaking me, you bad little thing!" cried Margy, pushing the girl into a chair and taking Helen's hand in both of hers. "I've got a position with the cutest, crankiest, dearest, awfullest little old lady you ever saw!"

"Now I know she's crazy," said Rose, with a helpless glance at Helen, but Margy interrupted impatiently.

"You are the crazy one. I never was more sane in my life. Listen," Margy leaned forward, her dancing eyes on the two eager girls. "Do you remember that ad that I told you I was going to answer as a last resort?"

"The one for the social secretary?" asked Helen, a little breathlessly.

Margy nodded.

"I didn't think that sort of thing was exactly in my line, and I don't know that it is yet," she continued. "But I told myself I couldn't afford to overlook anything, so I went up to Miss Pepper's address on Riverside Drive."

"Yes!" they breathed impatiently.

"A butler let me in! Oh, dears, the stunningest butler you ever saw, right out of a story book! He even dropped his h's—"

"Just fancy, a butler!" murmured Rose, in awe. "She won't be speaking to us, next."

" 'e took me right hupstairs and hannounced me," Margy continued, her mirth brimming again. "You've no idea how little and shabby I felt. I thought of my poor old year-before-last-year's blue suit, made over and dyed, and I wanted to sink right through the floor."

"I am quite sure I should have," marveled Rose, and Margy rushed on, intent upon her narrative.

"The sharpest kind of a voice in the room beyond said, 'Show the young lady in, Oliver.' Imagine that great big fat thing with the three chins being called 'Oliver'!"

"Like the trick bear named Hazel," mur-

mured Rose, and Margy turned laughing eyes
upon her.

"Exactly—only more foolish," she agreed.
"You would have to see Oliver to appreciate
the joke. Anyway, he let me in, and then I did
feel as though I would sink through the floor."

"You interest me strangely," proclaimed the
irrepressible Rose. "This Miss Pepper must
be a man-eater."

"Rose—such slang!" murmured Helen, but
Margy took no heed of either of them.

"She isn't a bit terrifying, really—just a little old lady with gray hair drawn back in a
fierce sort of knot at the back of her head and
with horn-rimmed spectacles that made her look
like an owl."

"What a lovely picture," murmured Rose,
and Margy grinned at her.

"It has to be seen to be appreciated," she
said.

Helen urged her on impatiently.

"But what did she say to you," she insisted.
Margy chuckled.

"Nothing at first—only looked. And I
thought that one look was going to put me out
on the street and farther from a job than ever.
I never have been looked at so disapprovingly
before. If I had been some stray cat that had
wandered in when Oliver left the door open,
she couldn't have looked more disgusted."

"Horrid old thing!" exclaimed Rose indignantly. "What right has she—"

"No, I won't have you abusing her," Margy interrupted, with a chuckle. "She is the dearest old thing ever, and really quite agreeable once she found out I wasn't a book agent.

"She thought I was at first, you know," and Margy began to laugh at the recollection. "She said, after staring at me suspiciously for fully five minutes, 'Well what is it this time, Bolshevistic Russia or Home Rule in Ireland'?"

"Imagine!" cried Rose delightedly. "Didn't you think she was mad?"

Margy nodded.

"For fully five minutes I was sure of it," she said. "My one idea was to escape to the safety of the street. Then I understood that she took me for a book agent and became myself once more."

"Did she ask you if you had had experience?" put in the quiet Helen.

"The very first thing!" admitted Margy, with a pained expression. "The very sound of that question made me so sick I thought I was going to faint. I shouldn't wonder if she thought so too, for she called to Oliver to push forward a chair. I happened to look at his face while he was doing it, and he looked so funny I thought I should scream. Imagine Oliver of the three chins setting a chair for a poor nobody like me with year-before-last-year's suit on her back and the dust of the street on her shoes. He didn't like it, I can tell you.''

''Pity about him!'' exclaimed Rose, indignantly. ''I'd like to tell that dancing bear what I think of him!''

''You never would,'' chuckled Margy. ''One look at him, and you would be scared to death.''

Rose snorted her scorn of this prophecy and Helen urged Margy on, impatient for the rest of the story.

''But what made her take you when you hadn't had experience?''

''Don't ask me. She was sorry for me, I guess,'' Margy responded, ruefully. ''Anyway, after she had asked me a peck of questions and found out just how ignorant I was, she snapped, as though she was awfully mad about something, 'All right. You'll do. Report for duty bag and baggage eight o'clock to-morrow morning.' That's one of the funny things about her. She keeps leaving out words all the time as though she were writing a telegram and every extra word cost money.''

''Eight o'clock!'' gasped Rose.

''But how much are you going to get?'' asked Helen, not so much interested in the eccentricities of Miss Pepper as she was in the details of this good fortune that had come to them. ''Did she tell you?''

''She did—and I almost fell over dead,'' replied Margy. ''Listen, my children and you shall hear! This darling old lady, this fairy godmother in disguise, is going to pay me thirty dollars a week—to start, mind you, to start!''

"And as for the finish, the sky's the limit," murmured Rose fervently. "Catch me, somebody. I am going to faint!"

"It—it's all wonderful," said Helen, and her voice shook a little in the blessed relief from gnawing anxiety and fear. "It seems too good to be true."

"Well, it is true, every bit of it," said Margy briskly. "And, just to prove it, look here!"

She opened a package which she had deposited unnoticed on the kitchen table and displayed to the famished gaze of the girls, a capon, cleaned and cut up and ready for stewing, fresh green peas shelled and attractive looking in their wooden container, and a box of strawberries.

The girls crowed with delight as they devoured this tempting array with their eyes, and Helen wasted no time in preparing the chicken.

Rose set about stemming the strawberries, but ate so many in the process that Margy, laughing, transferred her to the potato peeling, "for," as she explained, "they are not so tempting raw."

"Your Miss Pepper must have given you a whole year's salary in advance, if you can

throw money about so recklessly," Rose remarked, as she contentedly chewed the last
strawberry she had filched from the box.

"She gave me a week's advance," Margy admitted. "And when I stepped out of the house
with all that money in my pocket, what do you
suppose was the first thing I thought of?"

"Food!" guessed Rose, and Helen laughed
a little sadly.

"How hard it would have been for us a year
ago," she said, "to look forward to a time
when we should know actual hunger. Anyway," she added cheerfully, "we appreciate
a meal all the more when we do get one."

After dinner the girls became rather sober
and thoughtful. It had occurred to neither
Helen nor Rose up to that time that Margy's
connection with Miss Pepper would mean the
first break in their close trio.

"I suppose your new employer will expect
you to live with her?" questioned Helen, putting her thought into words. "A social secretary does, doesn't she?"

Margy nodded, and there was a mistiness in
her dark eyes.

"That was one reason I didn't want to answer the ad," she owned. "It will be horribly
lonesome in that big house without anyone of
—my own—"

"You will have Oliver," suggested Rose,
deceiving no one by her flippancy. Margy

chuckled and surreptitiously wiped her eyes. "Yes, I shall have Oliver," she agreed. "And now," she added, rising hastily and starting toward the bedroom, "I guess I'd better start packing. It won't take long," she added ruefully thinking of her pitifully scanty wardrobe.

The packing was done, the lights were out, and two girls lay side by side in the big old-fashioned bed that had belonged to their mother. The noises of the street came to them faintly, the heat oppressed them so that they could hardly breathe, and suddenly they were frightened, appalled by the power and ruthless-ness of the most fascinating and most terrify-ing city in the world.

For a long time they lay quietly, staring into the dark.

CHAPTER VII

AN UNEXPECTED LUXURY

THE night brought showers and relief from the intense heat.

In the morning the girls were in better spirits than they had been the night before and even the prospect of temporary separation from Margy seemed not nearly so tragic in the broad light of day.

Margy rose early, filled with the importance of her new position and determined to be on time for this first morning, at least. The eccentric Miss Pepper had said eight o'clock, and eight o'clock it would be!

Helen fairly forced her to eat a good breakfast of bacon and eggs and coffee, for excitement had robbed the girl of her ordinarily healthy appetite.

"I'll leave you twenty dollars of what Miss Pepper gave me yesterday, Helen," she said to the older girl, gulping down her coffee. "And I will try to save enough out of my salary to pay the rent."

"And in the next week or two Rose is almost sure to get some sort of position, even if it pays only a small salary, and I think I may be able to sell some of my sketches if I touch them up a bit," responded Helen cheerfully. "I hate to take so much of your money, Margy, when you need new clothes so badly."

For a moment Margy's face clouded, but she banished the expression immediately and gave Helen her gayest smile.

"I won't need much," she fibbed bravely. "And I would be pretty ungrateful if I weren't thankful that I am able to help out anyway I can, Nell."

At that moment came a shout from the youngest, and Rose charged in upon them, her eyes bright with excitement.

"What do you suppose just stopped before our door?"

"What?" they asked in unison.

"A limousine—a perfect peach!" Rose was fairly beside herself with excitement. "I bet it's for you, Marg. My goodness, just think of the style of us!"

"Oh, it can't be for me," Margy protested, half-frightened at the suggestion of such magnificence. "Miss Pepper said nothing about sending for me!"

But at that moment the buzzer in the kitchen rang with peculiar urgency and Rose ran to answer it.

Margy went excitedly to open the front door

and saw ascending the steps toward their apartment two men. The first she recognized as Miss Pepper's butler, that haughty possessor of the three chins. The second was a man in chauffeur's livery.

There could no longer be any possibility that it was a mistake. These men had come for her and her luggage to bear her like the princess in the fairy tale to the Prince's ball! That the Prince's ball in this instance resolved itself into the unromantic position of social secretary to a crabbed and exacting old woman, did not in any way detract from Margy's delight in the experience.

The trunk had been borne downstairs by the grunting and disgruntled Oliver—whose dignity had been sorely impaired by this menial task—and the man in chauffeur's livery.

Margy stopped behind for a moment to embrace her sisters tearfully and whisper that she would see them again just as soon as she was at liberty. Then she hurried down the stairs, obsessed by the fear of being late and thus offending her exacting new employer. Helen's last admonitions and Rose's excited comments and congratulations floated after her as she walked with a sense of unreality down the remaining flight of stairs.

She ran across the flooded sidewalk, not bothering to open her umbrella, and, still with that sense of unreality, entered the limousine whose door the chauffeur held open for her.

She gave the latter a swift glance and saw that he was a presentable young fellow, a few years older than herself, with sandy hair, blue eyes and a flashing smile. There was unfeigned, though respectful, admiration in his eyes as they rested upon her, and Margy wondered if she really was as pretty as he seemed to think her.

It was characteristic of Margy that she had never thought much about her personal attractiveness. Rose's beauty had always been her ideal of loveliness, and she knew that she was not at all like Rose. What she did not know was that, though of an utterly different type from her younger sister, she was, in her own way, very attractive and pretty.

Where Rose's skin was soft and creamy, hers was of olive tint. But the rich color that came and went beneath it, the dusky softness of her eyes, and the masses of lustrous dark hair, made a picture that many a passerby turned to look at twice.

On this particular morning she was even prettier than usual, for her color was high and her eyes sparkled with the excitement of her first adventure. She had become a wage earner! She was on the road to independence!

The thought in itself was inspiring and then —this wonderful car in which she traveled as though accustomed to such luxurious means of travel!

Ruefully she looked down at her shabby suit. Somehow, it did not seem to fit into the picture. Helen had been right; she needed new clothes dreadfully. Oh, well, later perhaps—

They had reached Riverside Drive, were drawing up before the imposing residence whose awesome interior she had timidly invaded the previous afternoon. Seen from this new vantage point, it seemed not nearly so terrifying.

The chauffeur opened the door and Margy stepped out upon the pavement. Her heart was beating rather wildly and she had an absurd impulse to dodge around the corner and seek the security of home and Helen's presence again. She was suddenly and terribly afraid of the erratic Miss Pepper!

Then she was in the presence of no less a personage than the lady herself.

The latter regarded her with that same frowning suspicious stare with which she had favored her upon their first meeting, and once more Margy felt as though she would like to sink through the floor, shabby blue suit and all.

Miss Pepper jerked a silken cord at her elbow, and the next moment a becapped and aproned maid appeared. She glanced at her mistress inquiringly, then looked at Margy standing as though rooted in the middle of the floor.

"Show Miss Blythe her room, Jane—blue room," she muttered, and without another glance in Margy's direction turned back to the litter of papers on the table before her.

The disapproving maid favored Margy with another insolent glance, turned and stalked out of the room.

Margy followed, supposing that that was the proper thing to do, but her blood was beginning to boil. Never of a very gentle temper, the insolent manner of this girl fanned her anger to a blaze. Perhaps it was the best thing that could have happened to her under the circumstances, for in the heat of her anger she forgot to be self-conscious or ill-at-ease.

Having ascended the stairs, the maid languidly flung open a door at the far end of a softly carpeted hall.

" 'Ere's your room, Miss," she said, with a barely perceptible pause before the "Miss." "I'll unpack your things if you like."

"Oh, no. I'll attend to my own things," Margy told her coldly. "You may go now!"

She hoped that was the right way to speak to a maid. Up to that time she had had very little practice.

Margy was relieved to see that the insolent maid was impressed by her manner. She withdrew, closing the door softly behind her, leav-

ing Margy to look about at the altogether unexpected luxury of her new quarters.

The decorations and draperies of the room
were in blue, and Margy had always loved blue.
The furniture was an ivory white and there
was a blue-shaded lamp upon one shelf of the
long-mirrored dressing table.

There was a door at the farther end of the
room, and, after she had taken off her coat
and hat and carefully put them away in the
closet, she went over and tried the handle of
this door.

It turned easily, the door swung open and
revealed a tiled bathroom, complete to the
closeted shower in one corner of it.

"I think I will pinch myself just to see if this
is really me," said Margy, forgetting gram-
mar and everything else in the surprise and
pleasure of the moment. "Imagine Margy
Blythe, out of a job yesterday, and owning a
bathroom like this all to herself the next!
Good gracious, I wish the girls could see it!
Wait till I tell Rose! Won't her eyes stick
out?"

After a few moments more of reveling in
the cozy luxury of her new surroundings,
Margy set herself hastily to the task of unpacking her few belongings. She feared the
sharp eyes and sarcastic tongue of Miss Pepper's maid more than she cared to admit, and
was not anxious that the latter should inspect

her modest wardrobe while she was on duty.

As Miss Pepper had deigned to give her no orders, she had not the slightest idea when her duties would begin. When her unpacking was done and still no word had come from below stairs, Margy sat down in the luxuriously padded and upholstered window seat to await developments.

The view from the window was superb, commanding, as it did, a view of the Drive and the river beyond it, but one could not remain satisfied with even so lovely a picture for an unlimited time, especially when one was as nervous and on edge as Margy Blythe was at that moment.

She asked herself why she should be nervous, but she did not have to search long for the answer. She was desperately afraid that she might not be able to please Miss Pepper and she was realizing for the first time how very anxious she was to succeed in this, her first position.

At this moment the obnoxious maid, without knocking, poked her head in the doorway to say indifferently:

"Miss Pepper would like to see you right away in the library."

CHAPTER VIII

Magic

MEANWHILE, there were Helen and Rose, still gazing at the dreary prospect outside the windows of the dingy little apartment far up toward the Two Hundreds and wondering just what they were going to do now that Margy was gone.

"It's a good deal worse for us than it is for her," Rose remarked moodily. "She will have all the excitement and fun of a new place and making money while we—"

"Ought to be very thankful for Margy's good fortune," Helen finished gently. "If this Miss Pepper hadn't happened to want a social secretary and chosen Margy—"

"To be it," Rose put in.

"To be it," laughed Helen, "things might be a good deal gloomier than they are to-day—now I'll tell you!"

"Sure! We got a good meal out of Miss Pepper, anyway," giggled Rose, adding impishly: "I wonder if that lady is as full of pep as her name. If she is, I'd like to meet her and—I don't envy Margy her job."

"I wish you wouldn't use that word 'job' so often," said Helen, as she turned from the window and began to tidy the living room. "It sounds so—common, someway."

"A rose by any other name would smell as sweet—or words to that effect," retorted Rose, as she picked up her hat and pulled it down over her bright hair. "I'd like to land one, call it what you may. How do I look, Nell?" she turned to pose impishly before her sister. "Do I look like the glittering business success that I feel like or the terrifical failure I feel more like. Come now, don't spare my feelings. Tell the truth at all costs!"

Helen drew her sister to her and kissed her gently.

"You look just like your name to me, dear," she said, adding anxiously as she glanced at the steady downpour of rain outside the window: "Must you go out to-day? After such a rain, to-morrow will almost surely be fair."

But Rose shook her head firmly. Her pretty mouth was compressed into a straight line of determination.

"I am going to get a job—excuse me, position—in the Lossar-Martin store to-day if it is the last act I perform on this earth. It's just about my last chance, and I can't afford to lose it. Wish me luck, Nell. I shall come home flaming with victory."

Then she was off, leaving Helen to stare at

the closed door and listen to her retreating footsteps as she sped down the stairs. The eyes of the older sister were wet as she set herself listlessly to the dull routine of house-work.

"It isn't right for me to stay here doing nothing, while they—and the two younger ones at that—go out and make money," she told herself rebelliously, as she finished the dusting and knew that her work was practically done for the day. "I could do something; I know I could, even if I have to give up my art for the time!" This last suggestion ended with a sob and, almost defensively, she brought forth her sketches and examined them critically.

"I could do some new ones, I suppose," she thought. "That might be better than trying to touch up the old ones. I ought to be able to find some good subjects in the parks—if I ever get time to go there!"

She turned again to the old sketches.

"They are really not so bad, after all," she reflected. "With a little touching up they might be made good enough to attract a buyer."

At the thought her eyes grew suddenly bright again. If she could find a market for her sketches, even though she were paid very little for them, she would be able to go on with her art studies—pay for them with her own money!

Two feverish spots of color began to burn on her cheeks as she got out her water colors and prepared her easel for work. She was so happily absorbed that lunch time came and passed without her knowledge. Not until the early twilight of a stormy day cast lengthening shadows into the living room did she pause to wonder at the swift passing of time.

"Rose has been away for a dreadfully long time," she told herself, reluctantly putting away her work. "I wonder where the child is. Nothing could have happened!"

But something had happened—something that was like an adventure in the Arabian Nights to Rose herself. The more she thought of it, the more impossible it seemed; and, yet, it had actually happened.

After leaving Helen with her gallant prophecy of victory that morning, she had gone straight to the Lossar-Martin department store.

She had avoided that emporium heretofore for the reason that the extreme elegance of its reputation had daunted her. She had gone past it many times, gazing longingly at its gorgeous and luxurious window display, had once almost entered within its magic portals. At the last moments she had fled, and ever since had been busily calling herself names because of that cowardice.

There was something about the very mag-

nificence of the place that overawed her, made
her conscious of her last year's dress and hat
and the patch on the sole of her shoe.

But to-day it was different. Perhaps it was
Margy's example of fearlessness in facing the
redoubtable Miss Pepper; perhaps it was the
fact that this seemed to be about her last
chance of placing herself with one of the larger
department stores. At any rate, be the reason
what it may, Rose decided to take her fate in
her hands.

She looked neither to the right nor to the
left in the damp and stifling subway for fear
she might see something or hear something
that would cause her to change her mind.

Once arrived at Forty-second Street, she
rushed toward the outer air, passing many of
her slower and less resolute sisters. Several
people looked at her and turned again to stare,
wondering what the very pretty girl was in
such a tremendous hurry about.

Rose gasped as she entered the magnificent
portals of the Lossar-Martin Department
Store much as an inexpert swimmer takes a
long breath before diving into deep and un-
known waters. But she never once wavered or
turned back. To-day it was do or die!

Her heart was beating violently when, after
meeting with determined opposition by various
clerks in the outer office, she finally found herself in the presence of the manager himself.

She had been given references by the minister of her church at home and by the president of the rather small and insignificant bank of Riverdale. The latter had been a friend of her father's and would gladly have done much more than that for the daughters of John Blythe. Rose clutched these two references with all the zeal of a drowning man who sees his one available log about to pass him by.

Mr. Paul C. Caruthers, bald, bespectacled and forty, continued to inspect the paper he held in his hand with frowning attention.

Rose coughed gently and he looked up—annoyed.

"Well, what do you want?" he snapped. "Who sent you here?"

"I did!" said Rose promptly. "As to what I want, I—I'd like fifteen dollars a week and a chance to earn it."

The face and neck of Paul C. Caruthers became purple, his eyes bulged. He half rose from his seat, then seated himself again, weakly.

"He is enraged," thought Rose. "In another moment he'll call all those smirking clerks in the outer office and have me put out. Oh, well, let him do it. I expected it."

Mr. Caruthers became still more purple in hue, coughed, stuttered, and—chuckled.

"Well, if you are not a conceited young person!" he exclaimed, and to the girl's incredulous ears he seemed amused. "What makes you think you are worth fifteen dollars a week?"

"I know I am worth much more than that," replied Rose, a smile breaking at the corners of her very pretty mouth. "But I'd be willing to start at fifteen."

"This becomes more interesting by the moment," Mr. Caruthers assured her. "Here, take this chair," he added, pushing one toward her. "I am eager to hear just why you think so well of yourself."

"I don't think so well of myself, really," answered Rose, becoming suddenly serious and looking at him squarely. "All I want to prove is that I am worth paying real money to for a real job."

"Any experience?" asked Mr. Paul Caruthers, suddenly hurried and businesslike again.

Now that question was like a red rag to a bull. Rose flamed at the great man as though he had offered her a deadly insult.

"No, I haven't had any experience! But I know that I can sell goods as well as any one else if I only have a chance!" she cried. "But you won't believe that and you won't give me the chance because I haven't had the experience. Experience! How does any one get it, anyhow? I—I'm sorry I've bothered you. Good morning."

"Hey, hold on there! What's the idea of going up in the air like that? I didn't say I wouldn't give you a chance, did I? Come back here, you little spitfire, and sit down in that chair and behave yourself!"

Rose hesitated. She was not accustomed to being talked to in that way and she was not a bit sure she liked it. But there was a humorous quality in the man's voice that made her do as he said. She came back slowly and sat down, her face flaming, her lips a little tremulous.

Paul C. Caruthers sat back in his swivel chair and studied her, finger tips together.

"You have pep and personality," he told her at last. "Two attributes that come in handy in just about every business, but most of all, I think, in the business of selling goods behind a counter.

"Now, I am going to give you a chance to sell goods," he said, leaning forward and looking at her sharply. "If you make good the sky's the limit—but it will be hard work. I am going to start you in the millinery trimmings department."

"Oh," said Rose faintly. "Thank you!"
Just then, it was all that she could say.

CHAPTER IX

New Acquaintances

Rose could have hugged the bald but genial Mr. Paul C. Caruthers with a good will. But, knowing that such a procedure was neither proper nor in good taste, she controlled the impulse.

As for the great man himself, having given orders to a black-haired, haughty young woman concerning Rose, he seemed suddenly to have lost all interest in the girl, turning back with frowning concentration to the reading of the letter which Rose's entrance had interrupted.

Rose looked sideways at the haughty young person as they stepped into the elevator together, and the latter condescended to grin good-naturedly.

"Startin' in right, girlie," she informed the half-elated and half-frightened Rose. "Took me three years to get to the artificial posies, and here you are steppin' right into the place the first thing. Paul C. must have thought you belonged with the flowers, or something. Say, girlie, is your middle name Rose?"

"No; but my first one is!" replied Rose, with a chuckle, and the haughty one's black eyes opened in a stare of unbelief.

"Gwan! now you're kiddin'," she remarked, but the stopping of the elevator at the third floor put an end to conversation and precipitated them both into a swaying mob of bargain seekers.

"Say, ain't this the limit?" said Rose's guide over her shoulder, as she deftly elbowed a way through the crowd to the millinery counter. "They've got some of our fancy stuff like feathers and velvet posies marked down to about half price. Note the riot!"

By this time Rose was thoroughly enjoying herself. She liked this slangy and ungrammatical, but good-natured, new acquaintance immensely. The thrill of having "landed a job" had whipped her cheeks to a deep pink and filled her eyes with sparkling imps of mischief. She was so buoyant and sanguine that even those in the bargain-mad crowd felt it and turned to stare after her admiringly.

Half an hour later found Rose installed in her position behind the millinery trimmings counter. Rose's partner behind the counter was the same black-haired and haughty young person who had guided her from the office of Paul C. Caruthers to her present comparatively lowly position.

Not that Rose considered it lowly. No indeed! She was to have many greater triumphs in the days and years to come, but none that would ever seem more important or thrilling to her than this first step on the ladder of success.

The name of her new acquaintance was Annabelle Black—a name which seemed very fitting to Rose, for Annabelle's hair and eyes could not have been blacker than they were and Annabelle's eyebrows were so black and heavy that they well-nigh met above her rather large but well-formed nose.

This girl was only a year or so older than Rose herself, yet she seemed years older; in fact, was years older in experience. Nevertheless, she was very kind to Rose, and the latter wondered more than once during the next few crowded hours what she would have done without Annabelle Black.

"You won't have to do much to-day, girlie," her new friend whispered to her during a moment when the milling crowd about the counter seemed to have thinned a little. "Just keep your ears and eyes wide open and let me and Birdie do the real work. To-morrow you can start in bein' a slave too."

The girl Annabelle had referred to as "Birdie" interested Rose immensely. She seemed such a quiet, demure little person, and yet she was so surprisingly efficient. More than once Rose found herself watching the movement of those deft fingers with something like fascination.

Birdie was small, with brown eyes, straight, wispy hair of a neutral tone, and a white, tired, little face whose expression of quiet endurance made Rose Blythe's heart ache.

Birdie was everywhere at once with a soft word for this frantic customer, a helpful suggestion for an undecided one, never cross, never snappy, like Annabelle, never insolent.

But Rose noticed—she had plenty of time to notice everything during that long afternoon, since she was permitted to handle only the smallest and most insignificant of the orders —that, in spite of her efficiency and good manners, Birdie was consistently snubbed, not only by Annabelle Black but by other girls at nearby counters. None of them worked half as hard or as faithfully as she, yet they made a great show of work and patronized the quiet girl as from some loftier plane.

This attitude both puzzled and angered Rose, for she had liked the quiet, mouselike girl at first sight and felt inclined to champion her. She became even more determined in this course after she met Mr. Herbert Shomberg.

Mr. Herbert Shomberg was a floorwalker, but one would have thought him, seeing him sauntering importantly among the aisles and counters of his domain, at least a king. He was a portly man and tall—he must have stood six feet two in his stocking feet. He was distinguished looking, too, and handsome after a fashion.

Because of all this, Rose was at a loss that first day to explain her strong aversion to the man.

He was pleasant to her, too. As he neared the counter behind which Annabelle and Birdie worked and she looked on, his roving eye happened to light upon Rose and he seemed to hurry his sauntering pace, shoving ruthlessly through the crowd of bargain seekers.

While the already overworked Birdie took complete charge of the trimmings counter, the black-eyed Annabelle proceeded languidly to introduce the "new girl."

Mr. Herbert Shomberg, while characteristically condescending, was genuinely impressed by the latter's good looks, and took small pains to hide the fact. He leaned over the counter and talked to her in a low tone, as casual and unhurried as though there were no frantic crowds milling about his elbows.

"I hope you will like it here, Miss Blythe," he began, and went on to say that she would be expected to attend the store school one or two mornings a week in order to master the rudiments of selling which she had not gained by experience.

Rose was eager to do this, as she was eager for anything that would advance her in her chosen work, and said so with enthusiasm.

Mr. Shomberg evidently approved of both the enthusiasm and the girl, and ended by shaking hands with her and hoping they would be the best of friends.

As he turned away Rose felt a little ashamed of her instinctive dislike of him, for he had certainly been very kind and encouraging. But the next moment something happened that immeasurably strengthened that dislike. It had to do with the quiet, mouse-like girl, Birdie.

All this time while Annabelle Black and other girls in the vicinity had been giving one ear to their customers and the other to the conversation between Rose and the floorwalker, Birdie had been conscientiously attending to her own business—and some of Annabelle's as well.

As Herbert Shomberg turned away from Rose, smiling benignly, it happened that Birdie handed a package to the wrong customer. She perceived her mistake instantly, but before she could rectify it, the woman to whom the package really belonged set up a hue and cry.

"That careless girl!" she cried, glaring at the hapless Birdie while Mr. Shomberg stopped to see what the trouble was. "If I had not had my eyes about me I would have been out a willow plume."

Birdie retrieved the package and handed it to the outraged customer.

"Here is your package, madam," she said. "I noticed my mistake as soon as I made it. You never were in any danger of losing your plume."

"The idea!" cried this unpleasant customer, rudely snatching at her plume and favoring Birdie with a parting glare. "You had better not be impudent, Miss, or I will report you to the management."

The woman was lost in the crowd and Rose noticed with pity that Birdie was trembling all over as she faced the annoyed frown of Mr. Herbert Shomberg.

"That is the second time you have made a mistake in one week, Miss North," said the latter, in a tone of severe reprimand. "If it happens again I shall be forced to take a complaint to the office myself." He turned away and marched commandingly through the mob while Birdie stared after him with a tragic white face.

"Well, ain't he the mean thing!" exclaimed Annabelle Black, as she put up a hand to rearrange her elaborate coiffure. "Always lookin' for trouble, he is. Just the same, Birdie," she added, with her patronizing air, "you'd ought to be more careful, you know. Think before you act is my motto in life."

It was late, and the bargain rush had thinned to a small dribble of customers before Rose had a chance to speak to the over-

worked Birdie. Then she waited until Annabelle was engaged with an exacting customer
before she dared make any overture.

"I wonder if you can't catch your breath
long enough to answer a question," she said,
in an undertone.

The other girl looked at her in surprise.
Then she smiled slowly and Rose was amazed
at the difference that smile made.

"I reckon I could," she admitted, "if it was
very important."

"Then why," demanded Rose, with a vehement sweep of her hand about the place, "do
you stand for the way people treat you here?"

The girl looked at her curiously for a moment, then smiled bitterly.

"If you had an invalid mother who depended
on your little bit of pay, maybe you'd stand
things too," she answered wearily.

CHAPTER X

A Real Celebration

Rose wanted to ask Birdie more questions, but at that moment Annabelle, the flamboyant, bore down upon them, demanding to know what they two were "jabberin'" about.

"You can go now, Posie," she told Rose—and by this variation of her name, Rose was to be known by the whole department. "You don't have to stay till closing time to-day. But see that you're on the job bright and early to-morrow A.M. We're goin' to have another sale like we had to-day, an', believe me, if we're not all dead before night, it will be luck an' nothin' else. Run along with you now. Me and Birdie's got to get back to business."

Rose started to say something, thought better of it, and closed her lips tightly. The last she saw of the two as she left the counter on her way to the employees elevator was a picture perfectly characteristic of them both. Annabelle was surreptitiously powdering her nose with the aid of a small hand mirror while Birdie North attended to two customers at once, keeping the peace between them only by the greatest tact and patience.

As Rose rode downstairs and stepped from the great emporium of Lossar-Martin, she was a prey to conflicting emotions. She was indignant with all her new acquaintances for the way they treated poor little Birdie North, she was aflame with the righteous desire to set things right at once. Then too she was tremendously thrilled at her success—and a little frightened as well.

Mr. Paul C. Caruthers had started her at fifteen dollars a week with the prospect of an increase if she proved as efficient as he hoped she would.

It was not a great deal of money, but it seemed like a small fortune to the eager and enthusiastic girl. Also, the promise of advancement was thrilling, like a bright light beckoning her on to the goal of her ambitions.

She felt, also, a little proud of her courage and determination. If it had not been for her pluck in bearding Paul C. Caruthers in his private lair, she never would have had the chance.

Her fear arose from the fact that she was not as confident as she had seemed of her ability to make a good saleswoman. Also, and this she found it hard to admit even to herself, she was a little afraid of Herbert Shomberg, the floorwalker. His manner to her seemed a little

too silky when she compared it with his tone
in addressing poor little Birdie North.

Rose possessed the gift of being able to esti-
mate pretty fairly a person at sight, and she
had very seldom known a first impression of
that sort to fail her. So now she believed that
Herbert Shomberg would be good to her and
helpful in every way as long as she pleased
him and did exactly as he said.

"Though I have never yet come at anybody's whistle, and I don't think I am likely to
begin now," she told herself, defiantly.

But thought of the floorwalker was unpleasant to her and she strove as far as possible to
put him from her mind. She had so far succeeded that by the time she reached the subway station she was smiling contentedly in
happy anticipation of the moment when she
should charge in upon Helen with the glorious
news.

She was about to disappear down the yawn-
ing well of the subway when a hail in a familiar
voice stopped her and she turned around, surprised.

A big moving van had stopped close to the
curb, and from it a young man jumped nimbly.
Rose recognized him at once. He was Joe
Morris, the young man who had helped them
in their moving and who had been so nice to
them later.

Rose felt a twinge of compunction as she remembered that they had repeatedly refused his invitations—had felt too poor at that time even to invite him to dinner with them.

But if Joe Morris had any idea he had been ill-treated, he certainly did not show it at that moment. He smiled delightedly upon Rose, showing his nice teeth, and she smiled back at him. He was much better looking than she had remembered him.

"Well, if this isn't luck!" he cried, as he held out to her one of his great brown hands. "All the time I've been looking around trying to catch a sight of you, and I couldn't. Now that I've just about given up hope, here you are!"

"I don't see why you had to look for me," said Rose, with the frankness of the present generation, while she shook the offered hand. "You certainly knew where I lived."

Joe grinned and Rose caught herself wishing he would do it again. It made his face look so nice and jolly!

"I got an idea I was about as popular as the smallpox around your house," he confided. "I don't know yet what I did to offend you, but even I can take a hint once in a while without waiting for the kick that goes with it."

Rose felt herself flushing with embarrassment. She could not very well tell this young fellow, nice and amiable as he undoubtedly

was, the true state of affairs. So she evaded
the question as gracefully as possible.

"We were awfully busy just then," she confided. "Getting to rights and everything, you
know—"

"Just as if I didn't take one whole half-day
to help you get to rights," young Morris reminded her reproachfully. "There's gratitude
for you."

They both laughed at that and Rose looked
at him, her head cocked on one side.

"You don't look like a person who holds a
grudge," she told him, adding primly: "We
dine at six-thirty. My sister and I will be glad
to have you join us to-morrow evening at our
humble meal."

She made him a mocking little bow and was
off down the stairs before the bewildered and
delighted Joe could detain her or even frame
an answer to her sudden invitation.

Meanwhile Rose was asking herself what
had possessed her to invite Joe Morris to dinner without even consulting Helen.

"I'll tell her my good news first," she decided diplomatically. "Then, maybe, she won't
mind when I tell her about Joe. Anyway,"
she added defiantly, "he is an awfully nice boy
and I like him."

Helen had just put away her sketches and
was starting toward the kitchen to get dinner

when the door opened and Rose flung herself
upon her.

"Nell, darling, the most gorgeous thing has
happened!" she cried, dragging Helen down
on the couch beside her, regardless of wet
clothing.

"You have a position!" divined Helen, an-
ticipating the glorious news.

"How did you know?" giggled Rose. "You
must have become a mind reader all of a sudden."

"Only one thing could make you look like
that," Helen explained. "Do tell me all about
it, dear. You know just how anxious I am."

Without further delay Rose launched into a
recital of the day's events and Helen proved a
most satisfying audience. Only once or twice
did she interrupt, and her enthusiasm was unfeigned.

They rejoiced together as Rose recounted
her experiences and were so absorbed that they
forgot all about dinner and were only reminded of the need for nourishment by the
pangs of imminent starvation; at least, so
Rose declared.

Gayly they got the meal together and when,
at the close of it, Rose mentioned her invitation to Joe Morris for the following evening
Helen completely surprised her younger sister
by seeming pleased that she had invited him.

"The house would be dull without a little

company sometimes," she said, adding fondly
as she looked at the pretty Rose: "And I
want more than anything else for you to be
contented and happy, dear."

Something caught in the younger girl's
throat, and it seemed suddenly to her as she
blinked through tears at her sister that it was
not Helen sitting there at all, but her mother,
with the old familiar smile on her lips. She
rushed around the table and flung her arms
about her sister, holding her tight.

"You darling old goose," she said huskily.
"You've got to stop thinking about other
people all the time and think of yourself a
little. You are the one who needs some fun
and good times—here alone in this stuffy old
place all day. And I'm going to see that you
have them, too!"

Helen laughed a little. It was funny to hear
that protective tone on the lips of her younger
sister; but it was very sweet, too.

They made a gala occasion out of next evening's dinner. They had fried chicken and
peas and a home-made cake that would have
made the finest chef in Paris green with envy
—this to quote Joe Morris after his third
piece!

They went to a moving picture theater after
dinner, the first treat of the kind the two girls
had had since their arrival in the city.

"Joe Morris was more amusing and delightful than ever, and there was only one thing needed to make this the end of a perfect day," sighed Rose, when the young man had gone and she and her sister were alone in the tiny apartment.

"And that one thing was Margy," agreed Helen. "If we don't hear from her sometime to-morrow, Rose, I think I shall have to take my courage in hand and brave the formidable Miss Pepper myself!"

CHAPTER XI

A Strange Employer

If Rose had been encountering unusual and exciting experiences in her search for a "job," Margy's life in the household of Miss Pepper had had its share of excitement and adventure.

The new social secretary was in the throes of something very like stage fright as she hesitated before descending to the presence of her new employer. She knew absolutely nothing about the duties of a social secretary, and while she had frankly told Miss Pepper this, she did not expect that lady to make allowances for her shortcomings.

"Well, there's one comfort," she told herself grimly. "I can die only once, anyway." And with this rather sorry comfort, she left the security of her room and slowly descended the heavily carpeted stairs toward the library.

She supposed this room was the one in which she had been received upon her arrival at the house, for there had been books, books, books in every available nook and cranny of it.

She remembered that this room was at the

front of the house and that heavy green portières hung before the doorway, concealing it.

She was hesitating before these same portières a moment later when the sound of a
quick step on the stairs behind her caused her
to look hastily over her shoulder.

The insolent maid was descending, and at
sight of the supercilious smile upon her lips,
Margy flung up her head and, without another
moment's hesitation, entered the room.

She found Miss Pepper sitting in exactly the
same spot before the littered table in which
Margy had left her, and she was bending over
a list of names with a frown of concentration.

"Can't make head or tail of the whole
beastly business," Margy heard her mutter,
as she entered. "Can't say want to, either.
Oho, so here you are!"

She whirled so quickly upon the girl that
Margy started nervously. If she had been the
veriest blackguard, Miss Pepper's greeting
could not have been more severely suspicious.
The new secretary found herself wondering if
there was any dreadful thing that she had
done and forgotten about later and that this
fearsome old woman had found out and was
holding over her as a threat.

Then Miss Pepper removed her spectacles
and Margy saw that her frown was caused
more by near-sightedness than bad temper.

"Come here, child," her queer employer ordered peremptorily. "Think I can see you if you stand off there? Unreasonable—very! Haven't the eyesight I once had, you know. Youth should be more considerate of age—really should!"

"I'm sorry," said poor Margy, feeling the accusing gaze of the old woman upon her and realizing a need for justification. "If I did anything I shouldn't—"

"Nonsense!" interrupted the surprising person irritably. "It's what you didn't do that I am talking about—not what you did. Come closer. I must have a good look at you."

Margy had the peculiar impression that she was living through one of the fantastic scenes in Alice in Wonderland. Certainly this peculiar old person could not be real. People didn't talk to you like that and order you about so in real life. Margy expected Miss Pepper to change into the Queen of Hearts at any moment and fly in her face.

But Miss Pepper did nothing of the kind. Instead, she subjected Margy to a prolonged and embarrassing inspection, at the end of which she grunted noncommittally.

"Looks well enough," she muttered to herself. "But you never can tell."

Margy did not know whether to be amused or angry. She compromised by deciding that Miss Pepper must be mentally unbalanced, and so not responsible for what she did.

For some time Margy sat in her chair by the window while the old lady went on with her business as unembarrassed by Margy's presence, apparently, as though she had been alone in the room.

The girl had begun to wonder resentfully if she had been employed for the sole purpose of sitting with her hands folded while Miss Pepper worked, when the latter rose suddenly from her chair, almost upsetting it as she did so, and turned spitefully, or so it seemed, upon her social secretary.

"There—you find out what's wrong with them if you can," she snapped, and, turning, walked briskly from the room.

For a moment Margy was too astonished to move or speak. She sat gaping at the door through which her employer had disappeared with a most inane expression upon her face.

"She—she must be mad—or I am," she told herself at last. She had risen from her chair, resolved to flee the house forever, when Miss Pepper returned as suddenly as she had left.

"Where are you going?" she demanded peevishly. "Set you to work, didn't I?"

"You certainly didn't, Miss Pepper," retorted Margy, becoming a trifle peevish on her own account. "You told me to find out what was wrong with something, and I have not the slightest idea what you meant."

Margy had no sooner spoken the hasty words

than she was sorry. She fully expected to be thrown out of the house without delay. What was her surprise then to see the seamed and wrinkled face of her employer break into a pleased smile!

"Good!" she cried. "Like you all better for spunk. Got lots of it myself. What is it you don't understand?"

"Oh—everything!" cried Margy, throwing out her hands in a helpless gesture. "You haven't told me a thing about my duties yet, Miss Pepper. I shall be glad to get down to work if I only know what there is to do."

"Most reasonable," announced her employer, with another pleased smile. "If there is one thing more than another I value, it is that quality of reasonableness. Yes, yes, of course you must know what you are to do before you can do it. Surely!"

All this time her hand was wandering among the litter of papers on her desk, stirring them into still more hopeless confusion.

"The trouble is," she looked up suddenly and favored Margy with a confidential smile, "I don't know anything more about it than you do!"

This was a poser! How in the world was one to guess at her duties in a new position if even her employer could not tell her what they were! She stood looking helplessly at Miss Pepper, and that queer person suddenly grinned companionably. It was the nearest she had come to looking human since the beginning of the interview, and Margy conceived a sudden liking for her new employer.

"Fact is," explained the latter, taking a seat and motioning Margy to do likewise, "had a most efficient social secretary for years—ever since I needed one, as a matter fact." Margy noted again that unusual trick of omitting a necessary word here and there. The fact that one's mind was continually kept busy filling in these omissions made it impossible to listen to Miss Pepper's discourse with any degree of quietness. It was very disconcerting, especially so to Margy at this time when she was so eager to learn just what it was this queer person did want of her.

"That was very fortunate," she said, as Miss Pepper stopped and regarded her severely, evidently expecting a reply.

"Quite!" she agreed dryly, making Margy feel she had said something very foolish indeed. "I picked her out myself," she added, with an air of triumph. "Homeliest creature ever set eyes on! Truly!" She beamed upon Margy, evidently expecting applause, but the girl was only mystified.

"I don't believe I quite understand," she confessed. "Why were you so anxious for a homely one?"

Miss Pepper frowned at such stupidity.

"So wouldn't get married, of course!" she snapped. "Silly habit—very silly. This one," she relaxed again and smiled in memory of her former secretary, "had cross eyes—terrible— and hook nose, regular hook nose. She had hair lip and funny teeth—spaces between 'em."

"I should think from that description," Margy ventured demurely, "you would not have had to worry about marriage in her case."

The words, innocent enough in themselves, seemed to annoy Miss Pepper past expression. She fairly leaped from her chair and regarded the girl with a startling asperity.

"Would you believe it?" she cried, and Margy realized with relief that her rage was for the departed secretary, not the present one. "She deserted me—got married!"

"Then," breathed Margy amusedly, "there is hope for all of us."

CHAPTER XII

Rex Appears

Miss Pepper stared for a moment, then broke into a shrill cackle of amusement.

"Aha, you have a sense of humor," she cried. "Best thing in world—sense of humor. Now let's get down to work!"

It was some time before Margy found out of just what this work consisted. Miss Pepper being rather vague on the subject herself, it was not strange that Margy should be mystified.

However, she came to the conclusion, after studying the litter of papers on Miss Pepper's desk, that her work would consist chiefly in reducing Miss Pepper's rather disconnected writings and peppery speech to letters in good social form. Also she would be expected to keep on file records of club meetings and data to be used at such meetings.

Having discovered this much, she plunged whole-heartedly into her work. Just to be busy was a relief, for during this first conversation with her employer, Miss Pepper had been un-

comfortably near to discharging her several
times, and Margy knew it. The eccentric Miss
Pepper might think she liked her now, but the
next moment she was quite capable of regarding her as her bitterest enemy.

"It will be about as comfortable as living
on the edge of a volcano," she thought ruefully. "You never know when it may start
erupting and bury everybody—including
Margy Blythe—in ashes two feet deep."

During the days that followed she came
more and more to believe that her first impression of the new position had been the correct
one. Miss Pepper was kind to her and considerate, in a rather extraordinary way, but
she was always asking unexpected questions
and expecting Margy to know by instinct what
things she wanted done without being told.

The brightest spot in her new life was
marked by the first visit of her sisters to the
home of Miss Pepper.

Margy was just entering her room late one
afternoon to freshen up for dinner when she
heard voices in the hall below. This was not
strange, since Miss Pepper often had late call-
ers. But these voices were raised as though in
altercation, and one of them Margy recognized
belonging to the pert maid, Jane. She turned
slowly from the door of her room toward the
stairway, and as she did so, heard Jane ex-
claim in her thin treble:

"I'm quite sure the new social secretary is engaged with the mistress's business and cannot be disturbed."

"And I am quite sure she will gladly be disturbed, if you will be kind enough to tell her we are here," said another voice, Helen's voice.

Rose was with her, for as Margy began hurriedly to descend the stairs she heard another familiar voice say impatiently:

"I'd like to know if you are going to keep us standing here all day?"

"No, Miss. Not at all, Miss," broke in another voice, and Margy knew that Oliver had appeared on the scene. She had reached the bend in the stairway and could see them all plainly. "If you will be so good, Miss, as to tell me your name—"

"These young ladies are my sisters, Oliver," said Margy quietly, and Oliver turned to her with an apologetic air.

"Quite so, Miss. Jane, here did not understand—"

What it was that Jane did or did not understand never came to light, for at that moment Rose flung her arms about her sister with a cry of delight.

"You old darling!" she cried, regardless of the indulgent Oliver and the supercilious Jane. "We thought we had lost you for good, Margy.

Now hurry and show us everything, for we've only a little while to stay.''

Margy hugged them both as they went up the wide staircase together, and for some absurd reason her eyes were full of tears and her throat held a lump it was hard to swallow. However, Rose kept up a running fire of comment that made it unnecessary for her to talk.

''Isn't Oliver a perfect lamb?'' Rose chuckled. ''You were quite right about his three chins, Margy dear. They are beautiful. But that dreadful maid! Jane, is her name? I don't see how you stand her about. I couldn't. Oh, Margy, you don't mean to say that you really live here?'' For they had reached Margy's room and the latter had flung open the door with an air of pride.

''It's mine,'' she assured them. ''At least, for as long as I stay with Miss Pepper,'' she added, so ruefully that Helen gave her a quick, anxious glance.

''Everything's all right, isn't it, dear?'' she questioned. ''You are quite happy in your work?''

''Oh, I love it!'' said Margy, with such evident sincerity that Helen was satisfied.

A happy time of inspecting everything and exclaiming about everything followed, and Margy began to feel at home in her new surroundings for the first time. If only she might keep her sisters with her always!

From the first Margy found her work interesting, and as the days went on and she accustomed herself to her surroundings she became very well satisfied with her lot.

It was not long before she found out, too, that, so far from being almost mad, as she had at first thought her, Miss Pepper was extraordinarily clever. She belonged to several worth-while women's clubs, was president of one and the chairman of an important committee in another, and was deeply interested in child-welfare work. As this last also interested Margy keenly, a bond of mutual sympathy and understanding strengthened their relationship, growing gradually into friendship.

Miss Pepper was interested in the girl's desire to become more proficient in her typewriting and stenography, and generously gave her a chance to gratify this desire by giving her all her evenings free. Margy immediately started a night-school course. This took up three evenings a week and left her the others to spend with Helen and Rose in the tiny uptown flat.

It was about two weeks after her entrance into the Pepper household that Margy discovered that her employer possessed a male relative.

Miss Pepper had never spoken of any family connections, and Margy had gradually come to believe that the maiden lady was alone in the world. But she discovered her mistake when Rex Pepper appeared on the scene.

Rex was about twenty-one, but he looked and acted scarcely nineteen. He was good-looking in a large-featured fashion, extravagantly well-dressed and carefully groomed. Margy never saw him when a hair on his sleekly brushed head was out of place or his tie awry. He had a grin too, good-natured and disarming, which he seemed never to take off.

Margy and Miss Pepper were seated in the library one day while the latter dictated letters to the various clubs in which she was interested when a sudden noise and sound of altercation was heard without.

"But she's busy, sir," came in Oliver's pompous but exasperated tones. "She left special horders that she was not to be disturbed."

"Oh, go chase yourself around the block, old porpoise," came in cheery masculine tones. "You know very well she will welcome me with open arms. I say, Oliver—my coat and stick. What, ho! are you blind?" The last was uttered in a tone of authority which evidently cowed the protesting Oliver. He was heard to murmur something about, "No, sir, not at all, sir!" and the next moment a grinning young giant parted the curtains and stepped into the library.

The expression of Miss Pepper had been growing gradually more forbidding in the last few seconds, but the newcomer seemed not to notice it. He walked right over to the little old lady, lifted her by her elbows from her chair, deliberately kissed her on both cheeks and set her gently down again.

"There now, you aren't going to be cross with your only beloved nephew, are you?" he wheedled, as Miss Pepper's expression remained stern and unrelenting. "Especially when he has just returned from a horrible cruise on a horrible yacht?"

"Can't you see I'm busy?" Miss Pepper snapped at him, by the barest perceptible gesture indicating her rather startled but amused secretary. "Are you blind?"

"Not at all!" retorted Rex, turning deliberately and letting his eyes rest with admiration upon Margy's flushed face. "I am in full possession of my eyesight, my dear aunt, and mighty thankful I am for it." Margy's eyes dropped before the admiration in his. For some reason she was furiously angry with him.

"A spoiled young cub, that's what he is," she thought resentfully. "And how I detest that type!"

There was a great deal more of the same kind of conversation between Rex Pepper and his aunt while the latter grew more and more exasperated and the grin of the former grew more wicked in the enjoyment of baiting the little old lady.

Time and again Rex Pepper made an attempt to draw Margy into the conversation, but she never once raised her eyes from the pad in her hand.

It was Miss Pepper who won finally, and she fairly shooed the lumbering, overgrown boy out of the library, for all the world, thought Margy, like a little belligerent hen pecking at a great, good-natured Newfoundland dog.

Miss Pepper came back to Margy, and without saying a word of this extraordinary invasion of her privacy, she began dictating a letter, then as suddenly stopped to question sharply:

"Well, what do you think of him?"

"Think of whom?" queried Margy, feigning ignorance.

"Of that great lumbering idiot of a nephew of mine," retorted the old lady angrily. "Whom suppose meant—Oliver?"

"I didn't know," retorted Margy, eyes demurely downcast. "You didn't mention any names."

"Well, aren't you going to answer me? What do you think of him?" cried the old lady, more irritably than before.

"Do you want to know my honest opinion?"

asked Margy, looking up at the old lady who
snapped at her in answer:

"That's what asked you, wasn't it?"

"Well, then," said Margy slowly, "I should
say that he was considerably spoiled and awfully conceited."

"Right!" cried the surprising old woman
delightedly. "I said you had brains. Come
on, now—work!"

For the next hour or two Margy was kept
so busy that she never gave a thought to Rex
Pepper. In fact, she had forgotten that any
such person existed when she was suddenly
confronted by the gentleman himself.

Miss Pepper had finished her dictation and
had gone upstairs to rest while Margy lin-
gered to rearrange some notes she had taken.
So she was quite alone when Rex Pepper put
in his appearance. A shadow fell across her
page and she looked up, startled, to see him
standing beside her. He seemed taller and
broader than ever and he still wore his amiable
grin.

"You aren't going to work any longer, are
you?" he asked, in the same wheedling tone he
had used with his angry aunt. "You really
shouldn't, you know—not on a day like this."

"I haven't had time to find out what kind of
day it is," returned Margy coldly, hastily
gathering up her notes in preparation for
flight.

"That's just the point!" urged this over-grown boy, evidently not in the least dismayed by her icy manner. "You shouldn't allow my aunt to make a slave of you. She's a kindly old soul, at heart."

It was on the tip of Margy's tongue to retort that she must be very good-natured and kind indeed to put up with such a nephew, but in the course of her short apprenticeship in the employ of Miss Pepper, she had learned to control such impulses.

Instead, she made no reply at all, she merely gathered up her papers and started for the door. At this Rex Pepper protested in an injured tone.

"You don't mean to say you are going to run away like that!" he cried, adding urgently: "I say, can't you wait long enough for a fellow to ask you a question?"

Margy, at the door, hesitated and half turned. There was something boyish and eager in his tone that, for the moment, disarmed her. Rex Pepper reached her side in two strides and looked down at her appealingly.

"I say, it's such a glorious day! Won't you come for a ride? The little old bus isn't much to look at, but it sure shows some speed."

"No, thank you," replied Margy, as coldly as she could. "I have some work to do."

"Oh, well, I suppose I should have expected that since I know what you think of me!"

Margy looked at him sharply.

"What do you mean by that?" she asked.

"Why," Rex explained, and he was still wearing his disarming grin, "I happened to overhear your private and quite plainly expressed opinion of me."

"You were listening?" Margy flared at him. "You were eavesdropping?"

"Not at all," protested Rex Pepper, looking pained. "I simply happened to be passing. But I say, won't you please change your mind and come for a ride?"

Margy swept past him with the air of a queen. She stopped at the foot of the stairs to transfix him with a look.

"I thought," she said icily, "that I had already answered that question."

CHAPTER XIII

Trouble

Margy's first encounter with Rex Pepper was ended. But it was not to be her last.

Fortunately, the young man did not live with his aunt in the Riverside Drive house. If he had, Margy would probably have been tempted to resign her position.

His father was dead, and his mother, an extremely rich widow, owned several homes, both summer and winter. At the present time she had gone abroad for the summer, and Rex, bored by many transatlantic excursions, had decided to stay at home for the summer and get acquainted with his own city under novel aspects. Now, because of Margy, he was thanking his stars for this decision.

Margy, wondering how anybody could be bored by too many trips to Europe, wished just as devoutly that he had gone with his mother and left her in peace.

Not that she altogether disliked him. He was good-natured and likable in many ways and his open admiration for her was as flattering as it was annoying. But she still considered him a spoiled and conceited youth who needed a good lesson to bring him to his senses.

Then, too, she was extremely busy and more than ever anxious to make good in her new position, so that she had no time to accept the young man's repeated invitations, had she so wished.

She was attending night school and becoming daily more proficient in the service of her employer. As far as she was concerned, the future looked very bright indeed, if only Rex Pepper would keep out of her life!

For Rose, it was a different story.

Her position was not turning out just as she had expected and hoped it would.

To be sure, she very soon accustomed herself to the routine of the store and found it more interesting than she had had any idea it could be. There were, for instance, the rest rooms for the girls. They were large and airy and comfortably furnished, the large chairs and couches inviting laziness.

"Though what time we have to rest, I'm sure I've never found out," Annabelle Black had grumbled in response to the surprised and delighted comments of Rose. "I think the management calls 'em 'rest rooms' as a sort of joke on us. It sure is a joke, girlie, take it from me!"

It was Annabelle also who introduced Rose

to the locker room and found her small, individual compartment for her. Rose did not like the locker room. It was long and narrow and rather dark, being lighted only by one window high above the floor. For some curious reason, the lockers, numbered and all in a row, made her think of prison cells. She became more accustomed to this room as the days went by, but she never quite succeeded in overcoming her dislike of it.

One thing that bothered Rose was the time-clock system. It had always been hard for her to be on time, and she was surprised to find how much difference five minutes made in the store routine. She struggled hard to overcome her tendency toward tardiness and succeeded so well that gradually the time clock ceased to be a terror to her and became merely a recognized part of the day's routine.

The real thorn in her side was Miss O'Brien.

This lady was the head of the millinery trimmings department who had not been present on the first day of Rose's apprenticeship in the department store, for the reason that she was just convalescing from a severe cold, but who had been very much present every day thereafter.

Miss O'Brien was a martinet of the most crabbed and unpleasant kind. She was one of those very efficient persons who continually go about with their noses in the air, hunting for trouble. And when one hunts for trouble, one is always pretty sure to find it. At least, Miss O'Brien did. All the girls disliked her, but she and Mr. Herbert Shomberg were firm friends. It seemed to be their special delight to harry and trouble the girls under their jurisdiction.

One day, in the midst of troubled thoughts concerning this same Miss O'Brien, Rose chanced to look across the intervening counters toward the elevators and saw a familiar figure. It was Helen. Rose flushed with pleasure and pulled at Birdie North's sleeve.

"Look!" she cried. "Here comes my sister! Isn't she the sweetest thing?"

Fortunately there was a lull in the push of customers about the millinery trimmings counter so that Birdie could give her interested attention to the slender, fair-haired girl approaching them.

"How pretty she is!" exclaimed the tired, patient little thing. "She is the one you told me about, the artist of the family, isn't she, Rose?"

The latter nodded and then turned to greet Helen with hands joyfully outstretched across the counter. Of course this tall, dreamy-eyed sister of hers had to be introduced to the girls at the millinery trimmings counter and to several other of Rose's new acquaintances as well. The girl was bubbling over with pleasure at

the unexpected visit and very proud of her
sister, too. She could see that all the girls
were impressed, even Annabelle Black. Then
several importunate customers charged down
to the counter and Helen knew it was time for
her to make her escape.

"It was dear of you to come," said Rose,
squeezing her hand tight across the counter.
"I wish you would do it often, Nell."

"I will," promised her sister, and was impatiently and almost rudely pushed aside by a
thin little old woman with thick-lensed spectacles and a terrific scowl.

"Attend to me, if you please, young lady,"
said this new customer, as Rose wistfully
watched Helen disappear among the throng of
shoppers. "If you will be so good as to bring
your mind to the subject of plumes—"

With an effort Rose focused her attention
on the speaker.

"What can I do for you, Madam?" she asked
automatically.

"You may sell me one of those willow
plumes if you will be so kind!" snapped the
woman, and Rose hastened to set a dazzling
array of the plumes before her.

"Not colors!" protested the queer customer.
"Suppose I want to deck myself out like cir-
cus clown? Ridiculous! Green, yellow,
orange, red—every color of rainbow! Show
me black ones!"

Rose hurried to set some magnificent black plumes before her customer, who, after considering for a short time, picked out one. There was something about the woman that struck Rose as familiar, but she could not tell just what it was till the old lady requested that her purchase be charged and sent to Miss Dorcas Pepper at a certain address on Riverside Drive.

Rose leaned forward eagerly, started to speak, but, with an abruptness that characterized all her actions, Miss Pepper turned away and was walking briskly toward the east wing of the store before the words came.

"That's Margy's Miss Pepper!" Rose said aloud, and Annabelle Black, overhearing, glanced at her curiously.

"Talkin' to yourself, girlie? Awful bad habit! I knew a fellow once said it was a sure sign of a weak brain. But say, girlie, who's your new friend in the black outfit?"

"Her name is Miss Pepper, and one of my sisters lives with her. A sort of social secretary, she is."

"Take it from me, Posie, I sure pity your sister," commiserated the older girl, but Rose chuckled delightedly.

"Oh, I don't know," she said. "I shouldn't wonder if Margy was in for a lot of fun, myself."

"Humph!" snorted Annabelle. "That all depends on what you like to call fun."

In the days that followed Helen's visit to the store and Rose's encounter with Miss Pepper, Rose found herself singularly free from the floorwalker's criticism and she wondered considerably about this until the sophisticated Annabelle Black pointed out that Rose was the prettiest thing in that part of the world and that Mr. Shomberg was not exactly "what you might call blind."

Meanwhile, Rose made one good friend in the Lossar-Martin store, and she was Birdie North, the quiet and efficient girl whom she had liked at first sight.

Birdie, whose real name was Roberta and who had been given her nickname by the girls in the store because she was "always hoppin' around," to quote Annabelle Black again, spent several evenings with Rose and her sisters in the Blythe apartment, and Rose, on her part, went often with Birdie to visit the little three-room flat where the girl and her invalid mother managed to eke out existence.

On one of these occasions Rose stopped at a restaurant on the way to Birdie's home and spent some of her hard-earned salary on a few delicacies for the mother of her friend. Birdie had once told her wistfully that Mrs. North craved chicken sandwiches with salad dressing, ice cream and roses. She had said that if her mother could once have all three of these things at one time, she would live happily ever after.

So, upon this occasion, Rose bought recklessly of chicken sandwiches, had a quart of French ice cream packed solidly in one brick, and, a little farther on, stopped at a florist's for her last and greatest extravagance—a half dozen exquisite tea rosebuds. The clerk, probably influenced by the flushed eagerness of his pretty customer, added a generous amount of ferns and packed the whole in an alluring green box. Feeling like somebody's fairy godmother, Rose proceeded to the Norths' apartment. Birdie opened the door and Rose pushed quickly past her.

"I've come to see your mother, to-day," she announced, making straight for the door at the end of the little dark hall which she knew led to Mrs. North's room. "May I go in?" she paused and looked around at her friend, who nodded emphatically.

"Of course," she said. "Mother is always happy to see you, Posie. It's Rose Blythe, Mother," she said, pushing open the door. "And it looks as if she had come bearing gifts, too!"

Mrs. North, in her invalid chair near the window, looked up eagerly as the two girls entered. Rose went straight over to her and, kneeling down beside the chair, took one of the worn hands in hers.

"I've brought you something I think you will like," she said, feeling suddenly shy in the presence of this thin, pale, patient woman. "Birdie said you like chicken sandwiches, ice cream and roses, and—and—here they are!" She placed the box of flowers in the invalid's lap, and, to hide her embarrassment, began to take the wrapping from her other two gifts.

Slowly, with an expression of wonder in her patient eyes, Mrs. North untied the ribbon about the florist's box and removed the cover. At sight of the exquisite buds in their nest of green, the invalid cried out softly, then buried her face in the flowers.

"Smell them! Oh, the fragrance of them! Smell them!" she cried to the two girls who were watching her with misty eyes. "It's like a little bit of heaven come down to earth. Rose Blythe, you dear girl, how did you know I loved tea roses best of all?"

"Birdie told me; and she told me you liked these, too!"

Rose pushed forward the sandwiches and the box of ice cream, and Mrs. North laughed suddenly and with the excitement of a child who has been given a new toy after a long, long time of no toys at all.

It was a wonderful party, and when Rose

tore herself away at last, Birdie followed her
to the door.

"Rose, did you hear her laugh?" she cried,
her eyes wide with wonder. "I would give—
I would give anything, everything, to keep her
laughing like that. And you did it, Rose
Blythe! Oh, Posie, I do love you!" For days
after that Rose could think of little but
Birdie's mother and Birdie's pitiful cry, "I
would give anything, everything, to keep her
laughing like that!"

Rose grew to love Mrs. North, who was always hopeful and cheery, despite her poverty
and invalid condition. As her affection grew
for both these new friends of hers, she became
more and more indignant with the girls at the
store—to say nothing of Herbert Shomberg
and disagreeable Miss O'Brien—who made
Birdie North's burden so much heavier than
it should have been. It was only Birdie herself who prevented Rose from voicing this indignation.

"It will make them all dislike you."

"As though I'd care!" cried Rose stoutly,
and Birdie looked at her with a wistful little
smile, wise beyond her years.

"Perhaps you wouldn't now," she said, with
a shake of her head. "But that's only because
you don't know how dreadful it is to be disliked."

"Well, if you think I am afraid to say anything I like," cried Rose, her eyes snapping, "you are very much mistaken, Birdie North! You just wait till the next time Mr. Shomberg talks to you as if you were the—the dust under his feet—"

"Oh, Rose, you mustn't say anything, you mustn't!"

Roberta laid a thin little hand on her friend's arm and Rose was surprised to see that it was trembling.

"Don't you see?" Birdie's eyes were wide with terror. "I might lose my position, and then what should I—what would mother do?"

Rose hesitated, staring at Birdie, angry and perplexed. She could see her friend's side of it, of course, but in her heart she knew that the whole thing was horribly unfair. Because she so desperately needed the pittance the store allowed her for her work behind the counter, the girl could not defend herself against cowardly attack, could not even allow a friend to stand up for her.

"Why—why—it's dreadful!" cried Rose, her blue eyes very wide. "It's like being a slave."

Birdie nodded.

"That's just what we are," she said grimly. "Slaves to a system."

How true that observation was Rose found out only the next day.

There was trouble—serious trouble at the

store. Among other things, upon the counter behind which Rose spent most of her waking hours, there was a collection of exquisite and expensive plumes.

Rose had sold many of these to wealthy and discriminating patrons of the store and she delighted in the mere sight and touch of them. She even indulged in a day dream or two about the time when she herself would be able to wear one of these luxurious and beautiful things. There was a blue one that she knew exactly matched the color of her eyes—

She put away these dreams resolutely, although they inspired her to work with a double fervor and to study with greater enthusiasm the fascinating work of buying and selling. Perhaps some day she might rise to the dizzy heights of buyer for the Lossar-Martin Department Store. That would mean—

But Rose refused to let herself think of all this would mean. She knew that it was necessary for her to learn to walk before she attempted to fly, and, very sensibly, she resolved to bend all her energies upon the building of a solid foundation for her future success.

But upon this particular day something altogether unheard of and mystifying occurred. A willow plume, one of the handsomest and most expensive, disappeared in some mysterious fashion from the counter.

Since these valuable ornaments were especially under Rose's care, it was natural that the grim-visaged Miss O'Brien and, later still, Mr. Shomberg, should look to her for an accounting.

Rose, perplexed and bewildered, could only reply in response to their increasingly severe questioning that she had no idea what had become of the plume. Except for the luncheon hour, she had been there constantly.

"You are sure no one could have taken it while your back was to the counter?" Miss O'Brien questioned sharply.

Rose looked her squarely in the eyes.

"I am quite certain I did not turn my back, Miss O'Brien," she answered quietly. "As you know, we have been very busy all day, and I have been right on this spot since the rush started this morning."

"I think we may dismiss the possibility of theft," Mr. Shomberg told the agitated Miss O'Brien. "By a customer, that is," he added, with a cold look at Rose which affected her like the glassy eye of a reptile. "Our detectives are very efficient and continually on the watch, as you know. I feel quite sure that an article of such value as this plume could not have been carried from the store."

Rose stared at him wide-eyed. What was it he was trying to imply. Of what was he tacitly accusing her?

Something happened to her heart and she

knew for the first time what fear was like.
Was it possible that they suspected her—Rose
Blythe—of taking that plume?

The lockers of all the girls were searched,
but nothing was discovered—not even a clew
that might lead to the mysteriously missing
plume.

When closing time came Rose wended her
way homeward with a heavy heart. Even her
righteous indignation at being suspected of a
crime she did not commit could not drive the
fear from her heart. If she could only forget
how Mr. Shomberg had looked when he had
spoken!

Anyway, she would not tell Helen and Margy
—not just now.

CHAPTER XIV

Helen Takes A Chance

Rose faithfully kept her promise to herself and did not tell either of her sisters of the trouble at the store. But only she herself knew how much this restraint cost her.

It would have been such a relief to have cried out the whole miserable story on Helen's sympathetic shoulder and have seen Margy's temper flash forth at this injustice. But they were having troubles of their own, as she very well knew, and she stoutly determined that she would not add to them.

As no trace could be found of the missing plume and as there seemed no possibility of placing the responsibility for its disappearance upon any of the employes of the Lossar-Martin Department Store, the affair gradually blew over. Nevertheless, Rose knew by the attitude of both the floorwalker and Miss O'Brien that they suspected her of knowing more than she had been willing to tell of the affair. She suspected also that she was being constantly watched.

All this did not tend to make Rose very happy in her work, and she found it increasingly hard to force herself to enter the magnificent portals of the Lossar-Martin Department Store.

Meantime, Helen was doing a great deal of thinking on her own account, and the result of it was eventually to bring a joyful surprise to the girls.

She had fixed up the apartment to the best of her ability, and the effect was good. Like her mother, she possessed the gift of making a little go a long way, and although the draperies in the little apartment were of cretonne, and not the best quality at that, the colors were so tasteful and pretty that the entire place took on a homelike air. Where it had been only one cubby-hole in a nest of similar cubby-holes, it became, through the older girl's ingenuity, a home.

But, having accomplished this much, Helen found herself at a standstill. The little flat was as pleasant and homelike as she could make it, and time began to hang heavily upon her hands.

She had her art, of course, but she felt that even in that she had come to a standstill. She had made a great number of sketches, some in water colors, some in black and white, but she felt that she was not qualified to undertake more ambitious work until she had had further instruction.

And to gain this longed-for instruction, she must have money!

To be sure, Rose and Margy turned over the bulk of their salaries to her, only reserving enough for daily expenses and the clothing they actually needed, but this was no more than enough to pay the rent of the apartment and furnish them with food and their living.

Helen went for comfort, as always, to her sketches and at last she found in them an inspiration also.

"Why not try to sell them?" she asked herself aloud, her voice sounding queer in the stillness of the orderly living room. "Somebody might think they were worth something. It would be better," she finished, with a little twist at the corners of her mouth, "than robbing a bank, anyway!"

Once resolved to try her luck, she became possessed by a feverish excitement. She searched through the sketches, selecting one here, rejecting another there, till she had what she thought was the cream of the lot.

So urgent was the feverish desire for action that she had dressed herself for the street before the thought occurred to her that she had not the slightest idea where the shops of the art dealers of the city were to be found.

"I'll look in the telephone directory," she

decided, and at that moment there came to her whisperingly from the past a recollection.

She had heard her mother speak of Dawson and Davis, a firm of art dealers whom she had highly respected. In fact, it had been the senior member of the firm who had been interested in her work before her marriage and had prophesied a great future for her.

If she went to this kindly man for whom she knew her mother had always felt the greatest esteem, told him of her relationship, and begged for his help in giving her a start—

But suddenly Helen's chin went up with a jerk and a look of resolution came into her eyes. No, she could not do this. She would stand on her own feet or not at all. If her sketches were not good enough to sell on their own face value, then she would never sell them. She would ask no favors of any one.

Several times during that trip downtown Helen's resolution weakened. She wanted success so dreadfully and it would help so to have an influential friend, interested for old times sake.

She was still undecided when she opened the door of the small but beautifully appointed establishment of Dawson and Davis.

There was no one visible when she first entered, and she had a moment or two to look about her at the beautiful paintings that adorned the walls or stood proudly upon easels

arranged so that the light might fall most flat-
teringly upon them.

Helen felt very small and insignificant and
humble amid all this magnificence. What could
Mr. Dawson, or Mr. Davis either, do with her
poor aspiring little sketches when they dealt
in masterpieces like these?"

In sudden panic, she turned, portfolio in
hand, and was starting for the door when a
voice at the rear of the shop brought her to a
standstill.

She summoned all her will power and turned
toward the voice. She saw a small, dapper,
rather insignificant looking man with hair so
tightly curled that it kinked all over his head.
He wore tortoise-shell rimmed glasses that
gave his light blue eyes a curious, twinkling
look.

"What will you have to-day, madam?" he
said, adding, ingratiatingly: "If I can serve
you in any way—"

Helen swallowed a lump in her throat and,
because the last remnants of her courage were
rapidly disappearing, hastily stated her mis-
sion.

Though the manner of Mr. Davis—she
learned during the course of the conversation
that Mr. Dawson was away on a business trip
—was as courteous and pleasant as ever,
Helen felt from the moment she began to open
her portfolio that his interest had waned.

Probably she was nothing more to him than one of the thousands of aspiring young artists in the city, and he was evidently prepared to find her work amateurish and crude even before she submitted it for his inspection.

Timidly Helen drew forth her precious sketches and laid them upon the counter. She was dimly aware that another person had come into the store and was peering over her shoulder. At any other time she would have resented this rudeness, but at the moment she was too wrought up to care about such a little thing.

Mr. Davis adjusted his eyeglasses, casually lifted one of her precious sketches in his hand. He inspected it for a second or two while Helen regarded him with imploring eyes, then turned to the next. He inspected them all, thumbed them over once more, then cleared his throat and looked at Helen.

"These sketches show a certain amount of talent," he said, moderately, while Helen stared at him, speechless. "If Mr. Dawson were here we might—er—talk things over. As it is—well—we don't specialize in things of this sort, you know." He smiled and made a gesture that was evidently meant to be affable and reassuring. "As I say, you show a certain degree of talent and, after a few years more study—"

He turned to a customer and Helen blindly

returned the sketches to the portfolio. What was it he had said? Oh, she did not remember —she did not want to remember! If he had only said they were hopelessly bad, she might have stood it. But praise like that—encouragement like that—

She turned swiftly away, eager to reach the street before the tears smarting behind her eyes could force past her control. She had almost reached the door when she felt a gentle hand upon her arm and turned, startled to find herself looking into a pair of kindly, twinkling old eyes.

"Well," the man surprisingly remarked, "you very nearly got away from me, after all!"

CHAPTER XV

Good Prospects

Helen stared at the old man for a moment in complete bewilderment, blinking back the tears of disappointment and humiliation.

"I—I don't think I quite understand," she said then, as the old man continued to regard her with his kindly, twinkling eyes. "Haven't you—made a mistake?"

"I think not—or, at least, I hope not," said he, adding with a chuckle: "I can tell better when I have a little closer look at your sketches."

At the words all Helen's misery and disappointment rushed back again in a flood.

"I—don't think my sketches will be shown again to-day," she said, softly. At her words the look in the elderly man's eyes softened to one of sympathetic pity.

"Youth always takes a first set back for the end of the road," he said, and gently led Helen toward the door. "If you will come to my little shop around the corner," he said, as, on the sidewalk, they stopped and faced each

121

other, "I think I may be able to make a proposition that will interest you."

Helen hesitated a moment, then walked on with her new acquaintance. Her breath came quickly as she asked:

"Are you, too, an art dealer?"

"Only a poor relation to Dawson and Davis," replied her companion, with his twinkling smile as he led her down a side street and opened the door of a modest little shop. "But for all that we have a reputation that we need not be ashamed of." Once inside the shop, the old gentleman turned to her with a friendly smile.

"Now, if you will let me see your sketches once again?" he suggested.

Helen complied, trying not to let herself hope too much from the friendliness of her new acquaintance.

She noticed that the latter seemed to care nothing for the sketches in black and white, but he took the several water colors she had brought with her and walked with them to the front of the shop where he could get a better light upon them.

He came to her again after a moment, smiling in his friendly fashion.

"You like them?" she asked, her voice scarcely above a whisper.

"I like them very much," he replied, adding quickly as he saw the swift flash of hope in her eyes: "Unfortunately, I do not buy sketches of this sort. However, I have other work that you can do for me if you are willing."

"And you will pay me for it?" cried Helen eagerly, and the next moment flushed with embarrassment as she realized the very mercenary sound of that question.

The eyes of the old gentleman twinkled.

"I have a habit of paying for work that is done for me," he assured her, and Helen hoped that, as he turned his back at that moment, he did not see her confusion.

He turned back to her, a bundle of prints in his hand.

"I have many of these to be colored," he told the wide-eyed girl. "And I have great trouble in finding any one who can do this work for me satisfactorily. But you are a true artist; you have a nice sense of color. In a few years I believe with my friend, Mr. Davis, you will have something to give the world."

Helen flushed again, but this time it was with pleasure.

"I am glad to hear you say that," she said softly. "I should like to be an artist more than anything else in the world."

"You are that already, my dear young lady," the old gentleman assured her kindly. "It remains only for you to become a great artist. Now as to these prints," he added, becoming suddenly very businesslike. "I will pay you a fairly good price for these," and he named a price that made Helen's heart jump with joy. "If these are as satisfactory as I think they should be from my observation of the kind of color work you do, I will give you more."

"There will be more?" queried Helen, feeling suddenly faint in the reaction from her discouragement.

The old gentleman smiled.

"As much more I believe," he said, "as you can do."

Helen was in such a daze of delight as she left the shop that she had gone almost a block toward the subway when she realized that she did not even know her new employer's name.

She retraced her steps, the heavy bundle of prints growing heavier with every foot of the way, but when she reached the store she was just in time to see the old gentleman disappearing around a corner ahead of her. She could not run after him, burdened as she was. She glanced up at the little sign over the door of the shop. There, printed in gold letters on a black background, was the caption:

G. W. Bullard, Art Dealer

She made a mental note of the number and turned back again toward the subway.

It was later than she thought, and she found

the subway jammed with perspiring humanity on the way home from work. Wedged in between a fat woman and a dusky-skinned Italian who smelled of garlic, Helen was forced to stand until she was within a few minutes' ride of her own station.

There she got out and staggered homeward with her heavy weight. She was eager to tell her triumph to her sisters and hoped that they would not have reached home before her. Rose generally got in about six o'clock, but when Margy had dinner with them she generally reached there earlier.

The walk from the station to the little flat seemed never-ending, and several times Helen was forced to put her bundle down for a moment while she rested her arm and regained her breath.

The next corner and she would be at home! Now she had gained it! If only the girls had not reached there before her!

Helen stumbled as she reached the steps just as a young man came briskly up from the other direction. The heavy bundle of prints flew from her hand, and she felt her arm clasped firmly while a pleasant voice said in her ear:

"That bottom step is a nuisance. It is only a half step, anyway, and ought to be abolished."

Helen gasped out an apology and looked at the owner of the pleasant voice. He had a fine face, thin and strong, and there was a humorous look in his gray eyes and about the corners of his mouth.

He stooped and recovered the package of prints, but as Helen held out her hand for it with a murmur of thanks he retained it smilingly.

"It is much too heavy for you to carry," he said. "Let me carry it up for you."

As he was already carrying out his suggestion and urging her gently toward the doorway, Helen had no alternative but to assent to it.

There was something familiar about his face she thought, and then remembered having seen this young man entering and leaving the apartment house on several occasions.

"Are you a neighbor of mine?" she asked on impulse, and the young man smiled.

"I am—if people in apartment houses can be said to be neighbors," he responded. They had now reached Helen's door and she felt hurriedly in her purse for her key. "I live on the first floor and my name is Draper—Hugh Draper," he told her.

"I am very much obliged to you, Mr. Draper."

The door flew open suddenly and Rose stood in the doorway.

"Good gracious, I thought you had deserted us forever—" The last words died off in a stare of amazement as she saw that Helen was not alone.

Helen introduced Mr. Draper to Rose, and, after thanking the young man again for his courtesy, said good-bye to him and followed the excited and talkative Rose into the apartment.

"Good gracious, where did you pick up that perfectly stunning man?" cried the latter, facing her sister in the small dining room. "Isn't he better than any moving picture hero you ever saw? And his eyes—did you notice them? Gray and dark-lashed. My, I'm crazy about him!"

"Don't be a little idiot," retorted Helen, smiling in spite of herself. "Probably Mr. Draper would be very much amazed to find that he had gray eyes and long lashes."

"Don't you believe it!" returned Rose, calmly. "I bet he knows all about it—and how to use 'em. But say, Nell, where have you been and what is this package?" She was nosing at the prints like an inquisitive young squirrel.

With an air of triumph she could not conceal, Helen told her of the day's happenings.

Rose whirled her sister about the room in a dance of jubilation and, as Margy's latch key was heard in the door at that moment, the story had to be told all over again.

They had a veritable feast that evening, and as Joe Morris happened in a little later, they finished the celebration by all going to the movies together.

Joe had become a familiar visitor by this time at the little flat, and Helen watched the growing friendship between him and Rose with some questionings. However, as he never asked the younger girl anywhere without including her and Margy in the invitation, Helen did not see how she could interfere.

Margy stayed with them that night, declaring that she must report to Miss Pepper early the following morning.

"To-morrow is her busy day—and mine too," she told the other girls as they were preparing for bed that night. "And if nobody objects, I think I will put the alarm clock under my pillow so that I can't possibly oversleep."

But in spite of her precaution Margy did oversleep the following morning. For the first time in its reliable history, the alarm clock failed to go off.

"I dread to go at all," cried Margy, as she dressed in an agony of haste. "She gets so terribly cross if any one keeps her waiting."

Rose jammed a hat down over her hair and turned to Margy with a grin.

"That just shows she's an old maid!"

CHAPTER XVI

SOMETHING WRONG

MARGY, alarmed at the prospect of her employer's displeasure, committed the unheard of extravagance of employing a taxicab to take her to the Riverside Drive house.

The ride downtown seemed a nightmare. Traffic policemen popped out at them repeatedly, seeming only to await the appearance of Margy and her cab as an excuse to tie up the long line of traffic.

They reached the Drive and Miss Pepper's home at last and, after paying the taxicab driver, Margy hurried into the house, her heart in her mouth. With any ordinary person it would have been easy to explain the reason for her tardiness. They would have had a laugh over the alarm clock's failure and let it go at that.

Not so with Miss Pepper. Upon some points she was as much a martinet as Rose's Miss O'Brien in the Lossar-Martin store. And she had a passion for promptness.

Margy's disquiet was not relieved by the fact

that she was met in the hall by the impertinent
maid, Jane, who announced that her mistress
had gone out several minutes earlier and had
left a message for her secretary.

At this moment Rex Pepper stepped from
the library, and, after greeting Margy like a
long-lost friend, turned with a commanding air
to the maid.

"I will deliver your mistress' message,
Jane," he said nonchalantly.

The girl hesitated, but Pepper had an air
with his aunt's servants that rather overawed
them. Jane hesitated another moment,
started to speak, thought better of it, and
finally left Margy and Rex alone.

"Come into the library a minute, Miss
Blythe," said the young fellow, holding back
the portières invitingly. "You needn't stand
there looking poised for flight."

Margy entered the library, then turned to
him in agitation.

"Will you please deliver your aunt's message at once?" she demanded. "If she has
gone I must follow her."

"That's exactly what I was about to sug-
gest," replied Rex Pepper, with every air of
sincerity. "I have my car all ready."

"Car! What has your car to do with it?"
cried Margy, puzzled and annoyed.

"Everything—as you will soon find out,"
retorted Pepper. "Now, Miss Blythe, this is

the idea.'' He leaned toward her. "My aunt
wants you to come out to the Blauveldt,'' nam-
ing a fashionable hotel on Long Island. "She
had to go there to meet some of her infernal
old club women, and she was very anxious to
have you come out there and take stenographic
notes of the meeting.''

Margy flashed him a look of suspicion.

"Strange she didn't say anything about this
to me yesterday,'' she said, voicing the suspicion.

"She didn't know anything about it until
last evening after you left,'' answered Rex,
still with that disarming air of sincerity. "The
shindig seems a rather important one, and
that's why she couldn't wait for you this morning.''

Margy was convinced at last, and she made
an impatient movement toward the door.

"In that case we had better be on our way,''
she suggested.

"Right-o!'' exclaimed Rex cheerfully. "As
I said, the good little bus is all ready and all
we need do is to step on the gas.''

He escorted her to the street with as much
formality as though they had been going to a
dance together and pointed out with pride the
natty little roadster that stood at the curb waiting for them.

"Just made for two,'' he observed, as he
opened the door and Margy slid into the low

seat. "You just wait till you hear how easy she runs!"

The car did run easily, and, under other circumstances, Margy would have enjoyed that run into the country immensely. It was luxury to sit in that comfortable, gently purring little speed car, to feel the wind on her face and to know again the joy and freedom of the out-of-doors.

She stole a sidewise glance at Rex Pepper and saw that he was better looking than she had thought him, now that he was doing something purposeful—if not particularly important. He returned her look and grinned.

"Having a good time?" he queried.

Margy stiffened. She was not taking this ride for a good time and he should have realized that fact without telling.

"It is pleasant," she admitted.

"But you're not taking the ride for your health?" asked Rex Pepper. "You're a wonder, Miss Blythe. If I were half as crazy about work as you are, I'd be a Wall Street financier by this time."

"Perhaps it would be better if you hated work less," remarked Margy, and Rex Pepper flushed under her glance. The next moment he resumed his usual good-natured grin.

"I see you have acquired my aunt's disapproval of me, Miss Blythe," he said, adding with a quick look at her: "Never mind, she doesn't hate me half as much as she pretends to; and you aren't going to, either, when you know me better." To this Margy deigned no reply.

From that time on until they were forced to stop and change a tire the girl kept her eyes straight on the road ahead and answered her companion's questions in the briefest of monosyllables.

"Say, that's hot work, let me tell you!" exclaimed Pepper, as he finished the exchange of tires and wiped his hands on a bit of old waste. "What say we stop for a little refreshment? A dish of ice cream or two—or six? There's a first-rate joy-dispersing parlor just a little way down the road."

His voice and his eyes were pleading, but Margy replied firmly in the negative.

"We haven't time," she reminded him. "If Miss Pepper is waiting—"

"Oh, hang my aunt!" exploded the boy, as he slithered into the driver's seat and sulkily started the engine. "Anybody'd think she was a Czarina or something."

"She is to me," sighed Margy, and again her companion favored her with a swift glance.

This time he seemed really intent upon getting her to her destination as quickly as possible. As they covered mile after mile of white road he kept his eyes ahead, seeming to urge every atom of speed out of the car. Margy leaned back with a sigh of relief. They must be almost there now.

"Here we are," said Rex Pepper suddenly.

Margy saw a long winding drive leading up to a picturesque rambling old building in colonial style painted white with green shutters. Rex drove up to the hotel and got out lazily.

"I'll hunt up the old lady for you and when I find her I'll deliver you to her," he said, and Margy was glad enough to assent to this.

There were several fashionably dressed people promenading the verandas, and Margy was conscious of her severely plain business suit.

Rex reappeared in what seemed an impossibly short time, and as he came over to the car his boyish face was a study. He looked at the same time anxious, triumphant, and apologetic.

"Well?" queried Margy, impatiently, sensing that something was wrong. "Did you find her?"

"She's gone," said the young fellow, adding, with a grin: "Guess she got tired of waiting."

Margy sat very still and her face grew suddenly white.

Rex Pepper climbed into the driver's seat and started the engine.

"Where are you going?" asked the girl, with stiff lips.

"Why, we might just as well go for a ride,

since business is off for to-day," he answered carelessly.

Margy turned upon him suddenly, her eyes blazing with anger.

"You will stop this car at once, Mr. Pepper. I am going to get out. If you don't stop the car, I'll jump out!"

CHAPTER XVII

JEALOUSY

THERE was no mistaking the fact that Margy was in deadly earnest. Rex Pepper gave her one quick glance and slowed the car, swinging over to the side of the road.

"What's all the row?" he was asking, in an injured tone, when a handsome limousine, coming from the opposite direction, slowed to a stop beside the little car.

Rex said something beneath his breath as he recognized the occupants of the big machine, a Mrs. Lane and her daughter, Gertrude, both intimate friends of Miss Pepper's.

The older woman was very handsome in a stout, florid way, and her daughter was a lovely picture in a soft-hued gray costume.

The latter leaned forward, shaking a finger roguishly at the red and embarrassed Rex.

"Thought you were dated to play golf with me this morning," she said in a voice, that, for all its levity, held a hint of threat. "We will play our foursome this afternoon, instead."

Rex, his poise regained, raised his hat in an elaborate salute to the young lady.

"I am grateful," he replied, grinning, "not only for the favor but for your forgiveness."

Gertrude Lane smiled upon him, gave his companion a sharp look, and the next moment the limousine purred up the road and was soon out of sight.

Margy, her cheeks flaming with mortification and wrath, fumbled at the catch of the door and Rex, humbly enough, opened it for her. She stood at the side of the road, her fists clenched and her eyes blazing.

"Who were those people?" she asked, in a low tone.

"Oh, just a couple of friends of mine and of my respected aunt's," he said carelessly, adding in an evident attempt to placate her: "I am sorry if they annoyed you."

"Annoyed me!" Margy repeated in the same dangerously quiet voice. "It is not they who have annoyed me. Oh, if I could tell you what I think of what you have done to-day—"

"Oh, now, I say," cried Rex, his face comical in its expression of injured innocence, "you act as if this was all my fault."

"Well, isn't it?" Margy flashed at him, and, turning, walked swiftly down the road.

Rex Pepper was out of the car in a moment and in pursuit. Reaching her he laid a hand on her arm and said in a curiously humble tone:

"Please don't go off like that. Won't you tell me where you are going?"

Margy shook the hand from her arm and turned and faced him, saying quietly:

"I am going to find the nearest train or trolley that will take me back to my employer."

"Let me take you back," pleaded Rex, but Margy replied coldly:

"No, thank you. I have trusted you enough for one day."

She turned again, and her manner was so finally one of dismissal that Rex Pepper stood helplessly in the road and watched her go. He turned then and walked back to the car, hands in pockets, a heavy frown on his face.

Margy had not much idea of where she was going or just how she was going to get back to the city. But she remembered having passed a trolley line a short way back, and she made toward this.

She walked stumblingly, so blinded by humiliation, anger, and anxiety as to what Miss Pepper would think of her that she scarcely saw the road ahead of her.

That Rex Pepper had planned the whole thing, had deliberately misrepresented Miss Pepper's orders to her, she did not now doubt. He had wanted her to ride with him on several occasions and he had probably thought this was an easy way to accomplish his wishes.

A caddish thing to do! She fought with the tears that stung her eyes. He had thought it smart, probably. A good joke—something he could laugh at afterward.

How was he, who had never had to want for anything in his life, to understand her side of the question, how appreciate the tremendous importance of her position to her?

It would have been bad enough if they had not met Mrs. Lane and her daughter. They had thought, no doubt—and, from appearances, they had every right to think—that Miss Pepper's secretary had gone riding with her employer's nephew when she should have been busy in her employer's service.

The faces of the two women had seemed familiar and now Margy was able to place them. They had come to Miss Pepper's one day to attend an informal club meeting and Margy had noted them chiefly because of the exquisite clothes they wore. She, Margy, had been present in order to take stenographic notes of the meeting.

Oh, yes, they knew who she was, well enough. And because Rex had slighted the girl by breaking an engagement with her, she would be swift to retaliate by means of the weapon in her hand. Oh, yes, she would tell Miss Pepper of the meeting!

Margy found the trolley line and was fortunate enough to catch a car immediately. The conductor proved to be amiable and talkative, and, as there happened to be only one other person beside herself in the car, he explained to her at length just how she could reach the city.

It seemed complicated to Margy, for she had to change to another trolley line before reaching the Long Island railroad and then to the subway after that, but she was grateful, nevertheless, for the information.

That journey was a nightmare to the girl. She had to wait interminable periods for cars and trains and all the time the vision of an angered Miss Pepper danced before her eyes.

She reached the Thirty-third Street station at last and darted for the subway, once more on familiar ground. Her progress from then on was gratifyingly swift, compared to the maddening delays she had met with along the line, and it seemed only a short time before the train drew up to her station.

She hurried to the street, but as she approached the palatial home of her employer, her steps lagged. Everything, she told herself, depended on whether Miss Pepper had already heard of her escapade—she used that term because it was undoubtedly the very word Miss Pepper would employ in describing the happenings of the morning.

Well, she would go in and brave it out, anyway. Perhaps her fears were a good deal worse than the reality would be.

She entered the house and was confronted by the superior and impudent maid.

Margy had at first wondered why this young person seemed to have taken such a violent dislike to her. Then, one day, she found out the real reason by accidentally overhearing a conversation between this maid and Miss Pepper's chauffeur. Jane had accused the chauffeur of admiration for the new secretary, and the chauffeur had been unwise enough to admit it. Margy gathered that the maid, Jane, was fond of the handsome chauffeur and furiously jealous of herself.

She had laughed at the absurdity of the whole thing at the time, for she had felt secure in the good graces of her employer. But now, as she faced the sneering girl, she realized that, innocently enough, she had made a powerful enemy in the household.

"Miss Pepper came in," said the girl in a malicious tone of triumph. "And when she found you had gone riding with Mr. Rex she went out to lunch. She gave me this note for you."

Margy took the note in trembling fingers and, with a cool glance at the girl and a murmured "thank you," turned toward the privacy of the library. There she opened the

note and read the one brief phrase it con-
tained.

"Report to me to-morrow morning at nine
o'clock.

"DORCAS PEPPER."

At any other time Margy would have smiled
at the sound of that name, for it seemed so
exactly to fit her employer. But just now she
was not in a smiling mood.

Nine o'clock to-morrow! And it was only
one-thirty! Evidently she had been excused
from duty for the rest of that day, at least.
To-morrow she might be excused from duty
forever, so far as her present employer was
concerned!

She left the house, discouraged and forlorn,
and, realizing that some of her fatigue undoubtedly came from lack of nourishment,
stopped in a little restaurant and ordered some
rolls and tea.

To-morrow morning at nine! And she must
wait all that time to know her fate!

CHAPTER XVIII

Other Plumes Gone

Margy said nothing of her fears to Helen when she reached the apartment.

She found the latter hard at work coloring her prints and so happy in the task that she was reluctant to spoil her pleasure. Besides, there was the possibility that she was making too much of the matter. When she explained to Miss Pepper—

But she had no chance to explain.

Facing her grim employer the following morning, Margy's heart sank. She knew then that there was no hope for her. She had offended the eccentric woman past all forgiveness.

"Trusted you!" Miss Pepper rasped out in her disjointed way. "Treated you like friend of family. Allowed you privileges. What did I get for it? Perfidy! Sneaking away with that worthless nephew of mine! Ignoring orders! Making the Peppers laughing stock! My nephew and my secretary! Nina Lane can well point finger at me and say: 'There goes foolish woman who trusted secretary!'"

143

"But, Miss Pepper," Margy broke in desperately at this point, "you may trust me, you may indeed!"

The older woman turned on her, her eyes gleaming dangerously.

"I have witnesses," she snapped. "Women who saw you and nephew. Don't make things worse. Don't falsify!"

Margy drew herself up, regarded Miss Pepper steadily for a moment.

"You do not have to say that to me, Miss Pepper," she said quietly. "I should not have tried to deceive you."

Without another word she turned and left the room.

Miss Pepper looked startled for a moment, the expression a strange one on her grim old face. She even half rose as if to go after the girl. Then the hard expression returned and she sank back in her chair.

"Better go! Little spitfire. They're all alike—the pretty ones. Like 'em better cross-eyed—hook nose. Oh, bother!"

Margy fled blindly toward the subway, her one desire to get home where she might give vent to her emotions.

Well, the worst had happened. She had been discharged—or had discharged herself. It was the same thing. Miss Pepper would have done it herself in another minute. She thought of Rex Pepper and clenched her fists.

"Something ought to be done to men like him! It isn't fair! They can have all the fun without paying for it! While I—" Oh, well, there was no use railing against fate. The thing for her to do now was to make up her mind what was to be her next move.

By the time she had reached home and had fitted the key in the lock, she was quite calm again.

There was no chance of keeping the bad news from her sisters any longer. She would have no more money and she would have to tell them why.

"Hello, dear!" It was Helen's voice calling cheerfully. "Another holiday, Margy? My, but your Miss Pepper must be a nice person."

Then Margy told her, breaking into a storm of sobbing despite her determination to do no such thing. Helen comforted her as best she could.

"As long as you know it was not your fault," she told the weeping girl, "you needn't worry, dear. There are other positions, you know; and you may find one that you like much better than this."

"Yes," said Margy, dolefully, sitting up and dabbing at her eyes. "I suppose I may."

Rose came in some time later with an expression that was determinedly bright. She, too, had to be told the bad news.

She was gallant about it and painted such alluring, though slangy, pictures of Margy's future that the girls were laughing almost light-heartedly when bedtime came.

But only Rose knew just how much that gallant effort cost her. She had managed to cheer Margy up a little, but how long, she asked herself, would it be before she would have to tell them of her own bad news?

Conditions were getting worse and worse at the store. The matter of the plume had blown over, but Mr. Herbert Shomberg was still openly and actively suspicious.

Besides that, several of the girls were jealous of her good looks and the attention she inevitably attracted and were trying in numerous ways to make life uncomfortable for her, as jealous girls know so well how to do.

Her two good friends were Birdie North and Annabelle Black. In spite of the latter's rather loud and boisterous manner, she was a good-natured and generous person and she admired "Posie" immensely. She even, at the latter's insistence, changed her manner toward Birdie North and deigned to recognize her existence.

These two made it possible for Rose to continue at the store. If it had not been for them she would probably have resigned her position, despite the fact that they were so desperately in need of her small income.

Meanwhile Helen had worked hard on the prints, doing her utmost to justify the old art dealer's opinion of her ability. On the evening after Margy's trouble with Miss Pepper, she submitted her finished work for the girls' inspection.

They were genuinely enthusiastic, declaring that if the old gentleman did not like them, they would have their own opinion of him as a critic. Accordingly Helen started downtown in high hopes the next morning, the bundle of finished prints under her arm.

The old gentleman had intimated that there would be more work where that had come from if she lived up to his expectations. Uttering a little prayer that her work might prove satisfactory, Helen approached the shop on the side street.

It had an air of desertion even before she tried the door and found it locked. She tried the door several times, thinking that, perhaps, it had only stuck. After a few moments of trying she was forced to admit that the little shop was really deserted, the door locked and the owner gone, no one knew where.

She stood there helplessly for a moment while a flood of disappointment threatened to engulf her. She had counted so much on that money and on the possible future work. What was she to do?

She studied the stores on either side of the

art shop. One was a beauty parlor, the other an electrical supply shop. It would do no harm to inquire in one or both of these concerning the whereabouts of Mr. Bullard. Perhaps he had only closed his shop for an hour or two.

On the wings of renewed hope she fairly ran into the electrical supply shop. She inquired eagerly of the pale-faced clerk who approached her whether he knew anything of the proprietor of the Bullard art shop. The youth shook his head in an indifferent negative but volunteered that the shop had been closed for a "right smart while."

Refusing to acknowledge her growing and terrible disappointment, Helen visited other shops in the neighborhood. Except for slight variations the information they could give her was all the same. Mr. Bullard had closed his shop and gone off—on a vacation probably— and a sensible thing to do in this weather.

Completely discouraged, Helen finally returned to the Bullard shop and stood there, looking at its inhospitable exterior and wondering wearily what she would do next.

Suddenly she thought of Dawson and Davis around the corner, and, after a moment of hesitation, decided to seek information regarding the old gentleman's whereabouts from them.

Mr. Bullard had been in the store that day when she had shown Mr. Davis her sketches. It was possible that they might know the old gentleman well and be able to tell her where he had gone and when he could be expected back.

But it did not take her long to find that this hope also was doomed to disappointment.

Mr. Davis, it seemed, knew the old gentleman rather well—he occasionally bought one of their pictures and was considered quite a connoisseur on art. But why he had shut up his little shop, where he had gone, and when he would be back, he had not the slightest idea.

She was turning away in complete discouragement when Mr. Davis, in an amiable mood, asked to see some of her work. Rather reluctantly she showed it to him and was relieved to see that he seemed impressed.

"That is rather unusually good," he said, and in spite of her disappointment Helen felt keen pleasure in the praise. "I have an idea that I know where you may get more work of the sort, if you care for it."

If she cared for it! Helen tried not to show how eager she really was as she asked for details.

There was a shop, it seemed, not far from there, whose owner, like Mr. Bullard, was looking for some one who could color prints satisfactorily. In fact, he had spoken of it that very morning. If the young lady would hurry——

In spite of the heat and the weight of the finished prints, Helen hurried.

She found the shop without difficulty, but

after exhibiting some of her sketches was told that they considered her work good but had nothing for her at the present time. They might have, later on, and if she would leave her name and address they would be glad to let her know if any such work turned up.

Utterly discouraged, Helen left the place and started for home. The reaction from hope, the bitter disappointment had filled her with a physical nausea, made her feel faint and ill. What would she do now? What could she do?

She reached the apartment, after a nightmare of crowds and subway trains, and found Margy there before her, returned from an unsuccessful round of place seeking.

"It's about the worst time in the year to look for anything to do," Margy confided to her elder sister, as the two girls set about the work of dinner getting. "Business isn't so brisk in the hot weather, and so many people are away on vacations that everything is all mixed up. If I could afford to wait till fall——"

Helen had hoped to hide her own misfortune from her sisters, but Margy had spied the bundle of finished prints before she had the opportunity to hide it and ferreted out the explanation.

"Anyway," Helen said, with forced cheerfulness, "it isn't as bad as if I had no hope of new work to do. I may hear from that new place in a few days and by that time perhaps Mr. Bullard will be back.''

For several days, while Helen tried to touch up her old sketches and things went from bad to worse for Rose at the Lossar-Martin Department Store, Margy haunted the employment agencies in her search for a position.

She found one at last, but the pay was poor and Margy knew from the start that she would find the work horribly dull and tedious. Still it was a position, and it meant at least a slight relief from their terrible money troubles.

As the days went by Margy became more and more discouraged with her new position. Her employer was an unpleasant, critical fellow who seemed to think it foolish to utter a word of praise for work well done. No matter how much Margy tried, it seemed that she could not please him.

And if he only would stop smoking those horrible black cigars!

Margy even dreamed of those cigars, and with every passing day grew to dread more the heavy, smoke-filled atmosphere of the office. Mr. Carter himself became repulsive to her. She could not bear to have him come near her. There were moments during his almost continual criticism of her work when she had a wild desire to start throwing things about the office. If only work were not so heart-breakingly hard to find!

One day, in desperation, she decided to write to Miss Pepper and tell her the truth about her ride with Rex. She did so, and for a week waited hopefully for a reply. When, at the end of that time, Miss Pepper had still taken no notice of her letter, she gave up any hope she might have had of reinstatement in her former position.

"I wish I hadn't written," she told herself hotly, fighting back tears of humiliation. "She probably doesn't believe a word I say, and I have only lowered my pride for nothing. Oh, it's a perfectly horrid old world!"

Although Margy said little about her new position and nothing at all about her unhappiness in it, Helen began gradually to sense that something was wrong. Margy was not looking well. She had lost her lovely color and her dark eyes seemed dull and lifeless. She came home night after night complaining of headache.

"It's those perfectly dreadful cigars Mr. Carter smokes," she told her sister, when Helen commented sympathetically and anxiously upon the frequent headaches. "If you could see them and the smoke he manages to get out of them, you would only wonder I could breathe at all."

While Margy continued to struggle on in her unpleasant position things began to happen to Rose in the Lossar-Martin Department Store.

Miss O' Brien came bustling up to her one morning looking worried and harassed and said in a voice from which the usual snap was missing:

"I wonder if you would go to the office on an errand for me. The girl has disappeared and I have a large new order to report. It is impossible to go myself and——"

"I'll go, of course," Rose agreed readily, and, accepting a printed slip from Miss O' Brien, made off in the direction of the office.

She performed the errand satisfactorily, and it was some little time after she had returned to her counter before she noticed that something was wrong. There had been four beautiful crimson plumes on her show case when she had left the counter at Miss O' Brien's request. Now there was only one!

She made guarded inquiries of Birdie and Annabelle as to whether any of these plumes had been sold during her absence, and both replied in the negative.

Rose was cold with fright as she faced this new problem. What had become of those plumes?

Certainly she had not taken them, and there had been no one near enough to her counter to have slipped them out when she was not looking. It might have happened, of course, during that time when she was forced to leave her post.

But one thing was quite sure: She would have to report the loss to Mr. Shomberg. And —what then?

CHAPTER XIX

Suspected

Rose felt she would almost as soon have put her hand in a hot flame as to have approached Herbert Shomberg on such a matter.

There was no doubt but that, considering his former suspicions of her, he would think her guilty.

Suddenly she flung her head up with a defiant gesture. They would think her guilty, but it still remained for them to prove her guilty. And they could not do that!

With that thought to strengthen her and give her courage, Rose quakingly approached Mr. Shomberg and asked in a low tone if she might have a word with him. Mr. Shomberg glanced at her sharply and immediately drew her into a comparatively secluded corner.

"If you have anything to say to me, say it quickly," commanded the fellow in his usual domineering manner, and Rose suddenly felt all her fear of him chance to an intense hatred. Her anger steadied her and she said in a voice whose coolness astonished herself:

"I have something very important to report, Mr. Shomberg. Three of our most valuable plumes have disappeared from the counter."

Mr. Shomberg glared at her for a moment in a terrible silence, then said in a freezing tone:

"Are you quite certain those plumes have not been sold, Miss Blythe?"

"Absolutely certain," returned Rose, giving him stare for stare. "I went to the office for a few moments—"

"And you are going to the office again," he cut in icily, "to explain the mystery of those missing plumes. This is not the first time such a thing has happened, as I think I need not remind you, Miss Blythe."

Rose turned away, not trusting herself to reply, and went straight to the office. She marched in, head held high, and stood before Mr. Beadle, the assistant manager.

The latter looked up, regarding her nearsightedly through his thick-lensed glasses. He was a small, thin man with a nervous habit of rubbing his eyeglasses when anything troubled or annoyed him. Ordinarily, he was good-tempered and kindly enough, but at this moment he seemed to Rose to rival the ogres of the fairy tales.

"Well, what **do you want**?" he asked, his

tone slightly impatient. "I am very busy, as you see."

Rose told him then, swiftly. Her face was hot and her mouth dry with excitement, but her eyes were frank and steady as she met the near-sighted ones of Mr. Beadle.

The latter's expression became very grave as she proceeded, and he fidgeted nervously with his glasses.

"This is unfortunate—very unfortunate, Miss Blythe," he said querulously, as Rose finished and stood, like a prisoner at the bar, awaiting her sentence. "It is not the first time such a thing has happened, and while we were inclined to consider the first occurrence a sales error, we can not do the same with this one."

He touched a bell and a girl appeared.

"Ask Mr. Shomberg to come here," he ordered, and Rose's heart sank within her.

The floorwalker appeared almost immediately. He glared at Rose for a moment, then turned his attention to the other man.

"You sent for me, sir?" he said.

"This loss of three valuable plumes has been reported to you?" the little man shot at him. "What do you think of it?"

Mr. Shomberg looked slightly taken aback, but he recovered immediately.

"I think it is more than mysterious," he said, with a significant glance at Rose. "If you will permit my saying so, sir, I should say that it was suspicious.''

''What do you mean by that?'' cried the harassed Mr. Beadle. ''Speak out, man— speak out. I have no patience with beating about the bush.''

Mr. Shomberg did not acutally ''speak out'' and say that he thought Rose was responsible for the missing plumes, but he succeeded in making his meaning as clear as if he had used the precise words, and seemed to take pleasure in making the veiled accusation.

Mr. Beadle favored him with a long, searching stare, which he bore with equanimity, then turned again to Rose.

''This is more serious than appeared to me at first, Miss Blythe,'' he said. ''I am sorry, but we will have to have your locker searched.''

Rose flushed crimson, but drew herself up proudly.

''I am perfectly willing!'' she replied.

They waited, Rose sitting stiffly upright in a chair, Mr. Beadle, after giving the necessary orders for the search, fiddling unhappily with his glasses. Of the three, Mr. Shomberg was the only one who showed no concern.

In a few moments one of the store detectives entered the office and said something in a low tone to Mr. Beadle. The latter turned with a relieved air toward Rose, though his face was still anxious and worried.

"Mr. Manning tells me that he has found nothing but your own personal belongings in your locker," he said, and hesitated, looking at her simple one piece dress with a critical eye.

Rose guessed what he was thinking—that it was barely possible she had the plumes about her person—and this was the last thing necessary to make her humiliation complete.

After that she listened in a sort of dazed misery while Mr. Beadle read her a lecture on carelessness and hinted that serious consequences might result if any other such mistake were made.

They released her at last, and Rose, crushing her hat fiercely over her pretty hair, dashed out into the street. Her one thought was to get away—anywhere, where she might be alone with her humiliation.

CHAPTER XX

Margy Is Sick

Because her eyes were blinded by tears, Rose bumped into Joe Morris without recognizing him.

With a muttered apology, she started to walk on when some one caught her arm and a hearty voice said:

"Say, what have I done to you, Rose? Aren't you going to say hello?"

Then Rose saw that it was Joe, and with an effort steadied her trembling lips.

"I'm—s-sorry," she stammered. "I wasn't seeing anything just then."

There was sympathy in Joe's glance as he took her arm and gently lead her toward the corner.

"Something has just about knocked you out," he said anxiously. "Aren't you going to tell me about it, Rose?"

The girl hesitated. At the moment she was not anxious to talk to anybody—even Joe. She wanted to be alone.

"I—must get back," she said, in a low tone,

not meeting his eyes. "I have just time to snatch a bite of lunch—"

"Capital! That happens to be my predicament, too!" exclaimed Joe, with his incurable optimism. "I know a slick little place right around the corner. Suppose we go there and diet on ham and eggs?"

Rose submitted to the inevitable, and before they had reached the restaurant she was glad that Joe had come along, glad that there was some one who liked her and still believed in her to whom she could tell her troubles.

Over the ham and eggs she told him just how conditions were at the store, told him, while he clenched his fists angrily, of the insinuations of Herbert Shomberg that she had been guilty of theft.

"The rotten hound!" he growled, adding as he leaned eagerly toward Rose. "Will you point this fellow out to me some time if I come to the store, Rose?"

Rose hesitated, looking at his ardent young face and clenched fists.

"You—you wouldn't fight him?" she asked, and Joe laughed shortly.

"Probably not in just the way you mean," he said. "Though I might do that under pressure. I don't mind admitting that it would give me one of the most joyful half hours of my life. But honestly, Rose," he added gravely, "what you have told me of this chap interests me. I would like an opportunity to size him up—and keep an eye on him.''

"Keep an eye on him?'' Rose repeated, puzzled. "I don't understand.''

"Probably you wouldn't,'' returned Joe, enigmatically, adding with a grin: "But I am willing to bet good money that you will before long. Look here, Rose, those feathers didn't grow legs and walk off by themselves, you know.''

Rose studied him for a minute and suddenly her eyes brightened. She even chuckled a little.

"Behold the great criminal detective, Joe Morris!'' she gibed, at which Joe grinned and thanked her for the compliment.

"And now listen, Rose,'' he said over the ice cream which he had insisted they have for dessert. "What you need is to get your mind off your troubles for a little while. There's a dance down at the armory to-night, and I was wondering if you would go with me. Thought I would be busy to-night and couldn't go, or I would have asked you before.''

"I—don't feel like it, Joe,'' Rose pleaded, the tears welling to her eyes again as she looked at him across the table. "It's lovely of you to ask me, but—''

"Now, listen here!'' Joe became suddenly forceful and Rose remembered afterward that she had liked him that way exceedingly. "You haven't got the right idea at all. Because you don't feel like it is the best argument for your going. It's going to be a classy shindig and, well—I'd like to show off the prettiest girl I know!''

This compliment, together with a great deal more persuasion, finally decided Rose to go to the dance, but only on condition that her sisters went too.

Joe was very glad to have them and said he knew two mighty nice fellows who would be tickled to death at the chance of ''showing them around.''

Almost in spite of herself, Rose felt cheered when she returned to the store. Ater all, it was not such a completely bad world if it held such pleasant things as armory dances.

When, later that afternoon, Joe dropped in and stopped at the millinery trimmings counter to buy a tiny cluster of velvet flowers—ostensibly—Rose was not surprised. When no one was looking she pointed out Shomberg, and was thrilled to hear Joe mutter beneath his breath:

''I thought so. Just the kind of chap I had in mind.''

He had to go then, hastily, for Shomberg was bearing down upon them with disapproval in his eye, but Rose felt comforted. For some reason she felt great confidence in Joe's ability to straighten things out for her.

When Rose first suggested the dance to Helen, the latter declared emphatically that she couldn't go, she hadn't a thing to wear!

"You have too!" Rose flatly contradicted. "How about that beaded white dress—"

"About five years old!"

"What difference does that make?" Rose insisted. "No one will be at the dance to-night who has ever seen it before. Wait a minute—I have an idea!" She fairly flew into Helen's room and the older sister followed her curiously.

Rose caught up the white dress from the closet, rummaged in a drawer for a moment, upsetting it hopelessly, and drew forth in triumph a bit of flesh-colored chiffon.

"Now put it on," she ordered, holding out the dress to Helen. "By the time I've draped this veil around you and added a pink rose, you won't know yourself—to say nothing of the dress. Now then!"

Helen slipped the dress over her head, frankly interested now, and Rose bent her bright head over the work of draping the veil artistically. She really did it very well and when she had added the pink rose from a collection of such pretty ornaments, even skeptical Helen had to admit that her work was good.

"You lovely thing!" cried the younger girl, hugging her sister without regard to the fragility of the rose. "You will be the belle of the ball, I know you will!" And before Helen could protest again that they really shouldn't go to the dance at all, Rose was out of the room and looking through her own limited wardrobe to find something that she could wear.

It was rather discouraging business, but she decided at last upon a blue organdy that might be made to do if it were neatly pressed.

When Margy came home a short time later she found her sisters flying around excitedly getting dinner. She was immediately pounced upon by Rose who, in one long sentence, told her the joyful news.

"But I have nothing to wear—" she began.

Rose clapped a hand over her mouth and led her in triumph to the room Margy shared with Helen. There on the bed was a dainty, cream-colored voile frock, not new, to be sure; but, carefully pressed by Rose's nimble fingers, it masqueraded quite successfully as a party frock.

Rose's enthusiasm was infectious and as they flew about getting dinner and clearing it away and helping each other dress, the color began to come back to Margy's pale face and she looked more like herself than she had for many a day. And when Joe, in company with the two young men of whom he had spoken so highly, drove up for them in a taxicab, it

seemed to the sisters as though their cup of enjoyment was full to overflowing.

Joe Morris brought the other two young fellows up to the apartment and introduced them
with a great deal of mock ceremony.

"This is Roy Reynolds," he said of a tall,
dark, good-looking chap. "He looks like a
bank robber but he is really quite a respectable
bond salesman."

"Bond salsemen are never respectable,"
drawled Roy Reynolds, and made his way over
to Helen's side where—it may be mentioned
here—he was to remain pretty steadily for the
rest of that evening.

The other young man was introduced as
Lloyd Roberts and, later, during the drive to
the armory, Margy learned to her surprise
that he was a brother of one of the girls who
worked in the office across from hers. This
bond of coincidence naturally made their acquaintance easy from the start.

After this auspicious beginning, how could
they help but have the times of their lives?

The Blythe girls became instantly popular
and their escorts were heard to complain more
than once that they wished some of these
"stags" had stayed at home where they belonged.

The dance floor was good, the music the best
of its kind and, caught in the whirl of enjoyment, the girls realized for the first time how

hungry they had been for dancing and good times.

"Oh, I don't want to go home," wailed Rose to Joe Morris, as the band swung into the suggestive strains of Home, Sweet Home. "That's the very worst of dances!" she added complainingly, as though it were all Joe's fault. "They always come to an end."

Rose found her two sisters no less reluctant to go home than she. But as every one else was doing it and the band was already dispersing, there seemed little else to do.

"I'm coming again," said Lloyd Roberts, smiling down at Margy as he said good night to her at the door of her apartment a little later. "If you won't let me come alone, I can always bring Betty as an excuse. My, but I'm glad you know my sister."

"So am I," replied Margy, demurely. "Betty Roberts is a lovely girl!"

When the boys had finally left them and they had let themselves into the apartment, Rose suddenly included both her sisters in an ecstatic hug.

"Now, you two old grumblers, aren't you glad I made you go?" she cried. " 'Fess up, now, wasn't it fun?"

It was fun, and that good time resulted in others for the girls, though they were forced to refuse many of the invitations showered upon them because they had not the money with which to buy the clothes necessary for parties and dances.

However, they did invite the young folks up to the apartment, and the tiny living room became gay with the fun and laughter of the boys and girls.

Annabelle Black became a frequent visitor at the Blythe apartment, and Birdie North came whenever her invalid mother could spare her. Although the latter never took much part in the hilarity all about her, she seemed to enjoy herself thoroughly. Her devotion to Rose increased until the two girls became very nearly inseparable.

At this time the Blythe girls could have been very happy if all had been well with them financially. But all was not well with them. The grim specter of Want dogged their footsteps, drawing a black cloud across the sunniest sky and keeping them continually anxious and worried.

Then, when things seemed at the darkest for the artist of the family, there came a feeble ray of light in the shape of a note from the proprietor of the art shop to which Mr. Davis had sent her on the day when she found the Bullard art shop deserted. The note informed her that the proprietor had a small order which he would be glad to have her take over if she could do so at that time.

Helen immediately hurried down to the store

and found that the order was a very small one
indeed. It would hardly be a drop in the financial bucket of the Blythe family. However,
Helen had reached the point where, if she
could not have the whole loaf, she was quite
grateful for the crumbs.

She accepted the small bundle of prints,
promising to have them done in a few days.
Leaving the shop, she went around to the Bullard store, hoping to get in touch with the proprietor. But the shop was still locked up. Its
deserted look seemed to mock her.

"Strange that he should have gone away
like that," she thought, as she wearily descended the stairs into the subway. "He must
have known that I would be coming back before long. He might at least have let me know.
I gave him my address. Perhaps," and her
heart sank as she uttered the possibility, "he
has gone away for good. Perhaps he doesn't
intend to come back again."

In another week the problem as to how to
meet expenses became really acute. The rent
of the apartment was so high that when that
obligation was met there was scarcely sufficient left to feed them for a month, and none at
all for clothes.

But Helen's chief source of worry was
Margy's health. The girl had no appetite,
though she forced herself to eat enough to keep
her alive and enable her to go on with her

work. She became painfully thin, and the shadows under her dark eyes made Helen's heart ache.

Margy should go to a doctor—that Helen knew. But how pay a doctor's bill? She remembered a tonic that her father had used and found extremely beneficial, and spent one of her much needed dollars in the purchase of a bottle.

Margy's eyes had filled with tears at sight of it when she realized how hard it was for them to spare the money, but she resolutely took the bitter stuff. It did not help her, however. She continued to lose weight and the shadows deepened and darkened beneath her eyes.

For some time past, Margy had had reason to believe that her employer was not doing well financially. If this were so, it accounted, perhaps, for the fact that Mr. Carter's manner became increasingly morose and unpleasant. His nagging and fault-finding became more and more unbearable.

Then one morning after Margy had been taking dictation steadily for over an hour in the smoke-filled office, she was suddenly attacked by a terrifying dizziness.

She rose to her feet, made instinctively for the window and, halfway to it, saw the world go suddenly black before her eyes. The solid floor gave way beneath her feet, red lights swam before her darkened vision and she floated gently downward through eternities of space. From a great distance she heard a voice say irritably, "Now, what do you think you are doing?" Then, nothingness—

"By cricky!" ejaculated Mr. Carter, staring at the limp form at his feet, "if that girl isn't the limit. Say," as he leaned down for a closer and somewhat startled inspection, "looks like she was dead!"

CHAPTER XXI

FACING WANT

WHEN Mr. Carter found out his mistake and saw Margy slowly flutter back to consciousness, his relief was equalled only by his fear that the next time this happened she might really die.

He certainly could not afford to have any one dying in his office. It would be unthinkable! So he gave Margy a week's salary in advance and sent her home in a taxicab—for good.

Betty Roberts, the girl who worked in the office across the hall from Margy and who, with her brother Lloyd, had been a frequent visitor at the Blythe apartment, went home in the cab with Margy.

Betty was a slight, appealing blonde who saw life in superlatives. She was using some of these superlatives now in ruthless condemnation of Margy's late employer.

"It's the worst thing I ever heard of, Margy, the very worst!" she stormed, as she rubbed Margy's hand between her plump little ones. "I never heard of such a thing—dismissing a

172

girl because she fainted! And in this heat too!
It's only a wonder we don't all of us faint. I
wish he would, the horrid old thing!''

Margy smiled faintly at this vehemence, but
at heart she was completely discouraged. She
was a failure all around, she decided. First
she had managed to make a muddle of her
position with Miss Pepper and now—this!
And, oh, how ill she felt, how faint and all gone
and utterly useless!

She began to cry suddenly from sheer weak-
ness, and the good-hearted Betty wiped her
eyes with her own handkerchief and smoothed
her hair and said dreadful things about Mr.
Carter.

They arrived home at last, and with Betty's
help Margy toiled up the unending flights of
stairs to the apartment.

Helen met them at the door, her face as
white as Margy's own.

Betty kept up a running fire of philosophic
comments on the beastliness of the business
world in general and of the Mr. Carters who
run it while Helen silently and efficiently put
Margy to bed. She pulled down the shade and,
coming back, bent over the relaxed girl.
Margy's eyes were closed and her curling
lashes were startlingly black against the pallor
of her face. Her mouth, pale too, was as tremulous as a child's. Helen bent down and kissed
her gently.

"Just rest now, little sister," she whispered. "I'm going to make you some lovely chicken broth. Just keep thinking of it and how good it is going to taste."

Margy put her arms about Helen's neck and hugged her tight for a moment, then turned over with a deep sigh, burrowing her head into the pillow.

The next morning Margy was very sick. In alarm Helen called the physician who had attended Birdie North's mother for a long time. Rose was so worried that she stayed at home from the store to hear the doctor's verdict. The latter arrived about noon, a kindly, gray-haired old gentleman who told them that Margy was suffering from a complete nervous breakdown.

"She must be kept very quiet, given a diet of nourishing and temptingly prepared food, and, above all things, she must not be allowed to worry. I imagine," he looked keenly at the two anxious girls, "that worry is the real cause of her trouble, combined with overwork."

"Oh, it sounds so easy!" cried Rose bitterly, after he had gone. "All he has to say is do this and do that. But you notice no one ever bothers to tell us how we are going to do these things. Oh, I wish Joe Morris were here!"

"Why, how could Joe help us?" asked Helen, startled out of her unhappy reverie.

"I don't know," returned Rose moodily,

adding with a wistful half-smile: "Only Joe seems to have a way of fixing things."

During the day that followed the howls of the wolf grew louder about the door of the tiny apartment.

Helen, leaving her patient to the care of a kindly neighbor, on several occasions, rode downtown, visiting every art store she could find in the hope of securing new work. She got some at last.

A week before Margy's sickness, the amount that the art dealer promised to pay her for the work would have seemed princely to Helen. Now, with nourishing and tempting dainties to be bought for the invalid and doctor's bill mounting up, it seemed only a drop in the bucket.

Upon one of his visits Doctor Marland looked Helen over professionally and offered a word of advice.

"If you don't let up on your own nerves, my dear child," he told her in his fatherly way, "I am afraid you will soon find yourself where your sister is now."

This prophecy filled Helen with terror. She had a vision of poor Rose trying to take care of two invalids and at the same time hold her position at the department store, and this pitiful vision did more to strengthen her nerve and resolution than any tonic could have done. She would not get sick—she could not!

She could not have told when a new anxiety concerning Rose crept into her mind. The girl never said much concerning her work at the store, but when she was questioned invariably answered that everything was fine.

But for the last few days she had been moody and silent, and once, when Helen asked if she did not feel well, she snapped out at her quite sharply. Of course, the next moment she repented and humbly begged her sister's pardon, but, try as she would, Helen could not forget the incident. Rose was unhappy in her work, things were not going well. What she at first had vaguely suspected gradually became a certainty.

Rose's happy good-nature was a thing of the past. She showed only a forced interest in things that went on about her, and this attitude was so foreign to her joy-craving nature that Helen became acutely worried.

She usually avoided questioning her sisters, for she had a dread of forcing confidences. But one night she could stand the suspense and uncertainty concerning Rose no longer.

The two girls were sitting in the living room, Helen busily darning a hole in her one pair of silk stockings, Rose moodily skimming the headlines of the newspaper.

Margy, who was sitting up every day now and for increasingly longer intervals, had gone to bed a short time before, complaining of a slight headache, so Helen and Rose were alone.

It was Helen who suddenly leaned over and put a hand on the younger girl's arm.

"Can't you tell me what the trouble is, dear?" she asked.

Rose, taken by surprise, looked up to see the tenderness in Helen's eyes, made a desperate attempt to hold on to her silence, and suddenly blurted out the truth.

The situation was far worse than Helen had imagined, and for a long time she sat with her arms about the younger girl, trying to think things out. At last she said, gently:

"I would advise you to leave the store at once, dear, and look for another position, but that would be rather like running away, wouldn't it?"

Rose looked up and studied her sister's face for a moment.

"I wouldn't get a very good recommendation," she said at last. An instant later she cried, with sudden wrath: "And I would like to stay and fight the thing out! I despise people who run away! I'll find out who is taking those things from my counter if it kills me!"

Meantime Margy was slowly getting stronger. She had responded to the rest treatment and the menu of delicacies provided by Helen.

Then, too, Lloyd Roberts had been attentive

to Margy during her convalescence. He had called frequently at the apartment, bringing books and magazines, candy and flowers.

To-day he had dropped in on his way home and had brought with him a box from the florist's and a pound box of candy, as well.

"Lloyd, you really shouldn't," Margy told him, as she took off the cover of the box and discovered a dozen roses. "These must have cost you a fortune. But, oh, aren't they beautiful?"

Lloyd Roberts smiled down at her, looking very handsome as he did so.

"I don't hear you enthusing so much about the candy," he suggested, and Margy made a laughing face at him.

"It's not quite as beautiful," she told him, gravely. "But I love it just as much!"

Rose, released from bondage at the store and arriving home just after young Roberts had left, gazed at the gorgeous bouquet of red roses on the table and from them to Margy's face, which was almost as rosy as the flowers. Then she spied the candy and lost little time in helping herself to some of it.

"Lloyd must be rich, or else he doesn't care what he does with his money," she said, adding with a sigh of utter dejection as she sank into a chair: "My, but I am tired!"

"What are they doing down at the corner?" asked Helen, at the window. "There have been explosions all morning, and one of them shook the pictures on the wall.''

"They're blasting for that new row of buildings they are going to put up," replied Rose disinterestedly, and relapsed into a gloomy reverie.

After a while Helen invited them both into the dining room, and there they saw, outspread upon the table, Helen's finished work, the last set of prints she had had to color.

"Oh, they are lovely!" cried Margy, in genuine admiration.

"The best you've done yet, old thing," added Rose slangily. "I don't see how you can get the sky and the hills and the trees blended so beautifully. Goodness! what's that?"

The sound of an explosion reverberated deafeningly in their ears. There was a ripping, cracking, rending sound, and it seemed to the girls as if the earth were descending upon them!

CHAPTER XXII

AFTER THE EXPLOSION

DOWN came the ceiling of the room upon the three Blythe girls, covering them with plaster and débris.

A descending slab struck Helen and hurled her to the floor. There she lay for a moment, half-stunned.

Margy and Rose were more frightened than hurt, and after a stupefied moment they ran to Helen's assistance.

"Helen! you aren't hurt?" cried Rose, as she saw the dazed look in her sister's eyes.

Margy, trembling with excitement and fright, knelt down beside Helen and began chafing her hands fiercely.

"It's that horrible old blasting!" Rose cried. "I've a good mind to go out there and tell those men what I think of them!"

Her vehemence roused Helen, who sat up and tried to smile.

"I'm all right," she protested. "Wasn't hurt a bit." Suddenly her gaze became fixed upon the table and froze into a horrified stare.

"Girls, look there!" she wailed. "My work! All my lovely work!"

The girls followed the direction of her shaking finger and cried out in dismay. The colored prints, the best work she had done and the result of many days of hard work, were covered under a mass of plaster.

Helen was on her feet, roused, for once in her life, to a fierce anger.

"It's an outrage!" she cried, rushing to the table and trying in vain to rescue some of the precious work. "They're completely ruined! I—oh, somebody shall suffer for this!"

Rose was at her side, shaking her excitedly by the arm.

"I know what to do," she cried. "Listen to me, Helen, won't you?" for Helen was still trying distractedly to rescue some of the pictures.

"That man downstairs," Rose hurried on, "that Mr. Draper, or whatever his name is— he's a lawyer—"

"How do you know that?" asked Helen, turning to her, her eyes bright, her lips set in a straight line.

"Oh, I don't know; somebody told me," returned Rose, impatiently, adding as she turned toward the door: "Shall I ask him to come up?"

"No, please don't," replied Helen. "I will go and see Mr. Draper myself."

It never occurred to her until after she had
left the apartment and was on her way downstairs that in all probability Mr. Draper was
downtown, attending to his clients. Luck was
with her, however, for the young lawyer had
just returned from his office and had stretched
himself out in an easy chair for a quiet afternoon of reading.

He also had been alarmed and annoyed by
the explosion, and was saying something un-
complimentary under his breath about the construction company when Helen's ring sounded
through the apartment. He abandoned his
book reluctantly and sauntered toward the
door.

All his annoyance vanished at sight of his
visitor, and he invited her within with the
greatest courtesy. But Helen would not go in.
Instead, she gave him a brief sketch of the happenings in her apartment and invited him up
there to see for himself the extent of the dam-
age.

Hugh Draper readily accompanied her, for
he remembered the lovely dreamy-eyed girl
whose package he had carried upstairs one
warm day and had more than once wondered
if that courtesy was sufficient to permit of his
calling upon this girl.

Now chance had come to his aid and had
furnished a real excuse for continuing the ac-
quaintanceship. Hugh Draper was inclined to

alter his opinion of the construction company!

However, he was genuinely indignant when he saw the damaged ceiling in the dining room, the ruined rug, and the spoiled prints on the table. And when Rose told him also that Helen had been struck by a piece of falling plaster, he vowed that the construction company should be made to pay and pay well for its carelessness, if he had any say in the matter.

"Then you will take it up for us?" asked Helen, a few minutes later, as she accompanied him to the door.

"I am very grateful indeed to be able to do anything to help you," the young lawyer responded, and Helen wondered for a moment why the look in his gray eyes made her so extraordinarily happy.

The happiness died away, however, as she turned from the door. Hugh Draper might make the construction company pay eventually, but what were the Blythe girls going to do in the meantime? That was the question! She had counted on the money from the pictures to help pay the doctor's bill. Now, instead, she would probably be required by the art dealer to pay for the ruined prints.

"Oh, if I only had some one to help us out now," she cried to herself sobbingly. "I don't —oh, I don't know what to do!"

At the store Rose came gradually to suspect

Herbert Shomberg of pilfering goods from her counter. It was suspicion only. There was no act on Shomberg's part of which she could complain to Mr. Beadle. But she noticed that he sent her on little errands, errands that in themselves were humiliating. She had not entered the employ of Lossar-Martin as an errand girl, but Herbert Shomberg seemed at times unaware of that fact.

Then one day after she had been absent from her counter for a considerable time on one of these errands she missed some valuable moiré ribbons. She reported the fact at once and was again forced to face the agitated Mr. Beadle in his office.

"You are certainly guilty of gross carelessness, if nothing else, Miss Blythe," he told her at the end of a humiliating interview. "We will be content to take this out of your pay this month, but if anything of the kind happens again I fear you will be asked to sever your connection with the store."

"Sever her connection with the store!"

How gladly she would have done so and of her own accord had conditions been otherwise at home! How gladly would she have flung her position in the face of her employers. She no longer cared particularly to vindicate herself. All she wanted was release from an intolerable position. If Margy could only gain strength and find work! If Helen could only get more art work!

If, if, if—always if! she thought, drearily. There was no way out of her predicament— none! She must simply stay and brave it out.

She continued to see Joe Morris frequently, and they formed the habit of occasionally lunching together at a small Italian restaurant where food was excellent and prices low.

Rose found relief in pouring out her troubles to the sympathetic Joe, but recently she had been puzzled and somewhat hurt by a seeming reluctance on his part to discuss her troubles at the store.

"Maybe I bore him, or perhaps he thinks I am just imagining things," she thought. "Anyway, he certainly acts that way." And being a proud girl, she decided no longer to force her confidences upon him.

Joe did not seem to notice her silence on the subject and, except for an occasional and apparently careless question concerning the doings and habits of Herbert Shomberg, he never referred to it himself. So Rose was completely taken by surprise one day when Joe Morris pushed and elbowed his way through the crowded aisles of the store and leaned over her counter.

"What are you doing here?" she asked him, almost severely, for she had caught sight of the floorwalker in the distance and was afraid

Joe's presence would only complicate matters.

"I've got to see the manager," whispered Joe, and there was a surpressed excitement in his voice that thrilled Rose in spite of herself. "Can you get me a line on how to reach the old boy at once without attracting any undue attention?"

Luckily Rose saw Mr. Beadle emerge from his office at that moment and start toward the elevators.

"There is the assistant manager," whispered Rose. "If you hurry you may be able to catch—"

Joe did not wait for her to finish the sentence. He was off like a shot through the crowd in the wake of the nervous Mr. Beadle.

Rose watched him, saw him reach Mr. Beadle and turn back with that gentleman toward his office. They disappeared together, and Rose drew a long breath.

"Now, what do you suppose is the meaning of that?" she asked herself, ignoring for the moment the insistent demands of a very stout lady in a very tight purple frock. Then seeing Mr. Shomberg bearing down upon her with the light of battle in his eye, she hastily turned to the irate customer, placating her with a dazzling smile.

"Who was that fellow?"

Rose looked up from giving the purple lady

her change and encountered the suspicious gaze of Herbert Shomberg.

"Friend of mine," she answered briefly, and immediately turned her attention to the clamoring demands of the next customer.

Shomberg flushed an angry red, opened his mouth as though to say something, then shut it tight again in a thin wrathful line.

"Say, Posie, but you must like flirting with your job!" It was the voice of the flamboyant Annabelle in her ear. "Old Shomberg has got it in for you, or my name ain't what it used to be."

Keeping one eye on Herbert Shomberg and the other on the office into which Joe and Mr. Beadle had disappeared, Rose waited on her customers in a daze. If they were given the right change or the right article, it was more due to luck than any attention on her part. After a while she saw Joe come out of the office alone and caught her breath in anticipation. He would come over to her—at least, give her a hint of what it was all about!

But in this supposition she was disappointed. Her heart sank as she saw Joe turn away and make hurriedly for the stairs.

Anyway, he would be sure to be waiting for her when she came out!

But he was not, and Rose was conscious of a mingling of emotions as she rode uptown in the inevitable business crush. Chief among them

was exasperation at Joe. What right had he
to get her all excited and then make no explanation of his peculiar actions? Well, the
next time she saw him she would tell him a
thing or two!

As she entered the apartment, Helen held
out an envelope to her.

"I found this pushed under the door," she
explained. "I don't know who left it, but the
writing on the envelope looks like Joe
Morris's."

With eager fingers Rose opened the note.
She pulled out a sheet of paper over which
was scrawled hastily:

"Keep your eyes open! In a day or two I
will ask you to compliment me on my ability in
detecting crime. Just sit tight and watch!

"JOE."

CHAPTER XXIII

Mystery

Meanwhile Margy felt so much improved in health that she declared herself ready to look for another position.

Helen protested, and begged her to wait until the hot weather was over. But Margy, knowing the true state of finances at home, was stubborn in her determination not to be a burden to her sisters one moment longer than necessary.

However, she swiftly found that her strength had not yet fully returned and that her sense of well being had been deceptive. After a day or two of the dreary rounds of employment agencies and cluttered offices she was forced to yield to Helen's plea that she be sensible and not overexert herself until her strength and the cooler weather returned.

"I'm just no good to anybody," she told herself bitterly. "I thought I was so strong and so capable, and now—look at me! Not able to do as much as Rose, who looks as if she would float away if you puffed hard at her."

She thought once more of writing to Miss
Pepper, but her pride would not let her do
that.   Her one letter had remained unan-
swered, and that was affront enough.

Had she known that Miss Pepper had left
town shortly after she had dismissed her secretary from her employ, and had never received the letter, Margy might have felt very
differently about a second attempt.   But she
did not know.

It had gotten so desperate with Helen that,
after paying a little on the doctor's bill and re-
embursing the art dealer for his ruined prints,
she had scarcely enough left in the budget to
provide the scantiest of meals for the week.

She hid her terrible anxiety from her sisters
as best she could, going about all day with a
smiling face and only at night giving way a
little to her fears for the future.

Hugh Draper had called once after his promise of assistance, and once again Helen was
conscious of that queer contentment in his
presence.   He told her that he was ''camping
on the trail'' of the construction company and
confidently promised results in a few days.

But, thought Helen, in the meantime—

And then, suddenly, out of a clear sky, or,
rather, a clouded one, things began to happen
—many things.

It began with Rose.

The latter, indignant as she was with Joe

for making no attempt to see her and explain his note and expecting any minute that he would so explain, was too absorbed in her own thoughts and conjectures to notice that Mr. Shomberg's enmity toward her was assuming more definite form.

Once or twice in conversation with her he had practically accused her of purloining the store's goods, and this in the hearing of her associates.

Once Birdie North had resented the insinuation fiercely and if Mr. Shomberg had not been completely taken aback by this assault from an unexpected quarter, she would probably have been discharged then and there. As it was, his manner toward her became so openly hostile that it began to look as though both she and Rose would be out of a position before the end of the week.

Then came the climax.

Again valuable plumes were missing from the millinery department, and this time the situation looked deadly serious for Rose. It began to seem that the severing of her connection with the Lossar-Martin company was the least that would happen to her.

The store was in an uproar—at least, that portion of it affected by this new and exciting development. There were those unfriendly to Rose who gathered in groups and declared that now that "uppy Rose Blythe would get all that was coming to her."

Rose, white and shaken, believed that they were right. In a daze she followed the sardonic Shomberg toward the assistant manager's office.

"The way ought to be very familiar to me by this time," she thought bitterly. "I've trodden it often enough!"

Shomberg stopped suddenly and Rose saw that a man had come up to him. Her heart fairly stopped beating as she recognized one of the store detectives.

Clerks at near-by counters sensed the tense drama of the situation and served their customers with divided attention.

The detective, instead of addressing himself directly to the floorwalker, turned to the white and quaking Rose.

"We found one of the plumes in your locker, Miss Blythe," he said abruptly.

Rose felt the room wheeling about her and the one thing that stood out clearly was Shomberg's face and the sneering expression on it.

"I knew it!" he cried. "I suspected this young woman from the first. Now we have the proof!"

As he uttered the words Rose tried desperately to think. What did this mean? What would they do to her? The evidence of this

plume in her locker seemed final. They might
—oh, they might send her to prison!

She felt herself stifling, wanted to cry out
wildly for air. It seemed to her that she could
feel the detective's hand upon her arm, the
hideous grip of the law!

"Not quite so fast, Mr. Shomberg!"

Rose looked up, startled at some unusual
quality in the detective's tone.

The latter was not looking at her at all. His
eyes were as cold as steel as he gazed at the
suddenly pale Shomberg.

"You want to be a little careful how you ac-
cuse any one."

"But you have the proof!" cried the floorwalker, and Rose thought she could detect a
hint of panic beneath the bluster of his tone.
"You say that you found one of the stolen
plumes in her locker."

"Yes. But, for all that, she is not the guilty
one. Come, Mr. Shomberg!" As Rose
watched, dazed and incredulous, the detective
put a hand upon the arm of Herbert Shomberg
and urged him gently toward the elevators.

The latter turned a ghastly greenish-gray
and cast a wild glance over his shoulder, as
though contemplating flight.

"Why, man, you're crazy!" he protested in
a last attempt at bluster. "It's all a ridiculous
mistake!"

"All right," interrupted the detective, his

hand tightening on his prisoner's arm. "You will have all the chance you need to tell 'em about it at headquarters. Will you come along quietly now or must I—"

Rose did not hear the end of the sentence for the reason that the two had disappeared from sight. Evidently Herbert Shomberg had decided to "go peaceably."

Weak and giddy with the reaction from terrible fear, Rose returned to her counter to be met by a volley of excited and eager questions. To all of them she shook her head dazedly.

"You know as much about it as I do," she said, and that was all they could get out of her.

It seemed an interminable age, during which Rose went about her business mechanically, before they sent for her at the office.

She went in fear and trembling, not trusting yet to her good fortune, half fearing that they had trumped up some new charge against her.

But she needed only one glance at the face of the beaming Mr. Beadle to tell her that her fears were groundless. He motioned her to a chair as though she had been a queen and proceeded to give her his whole attention.

He told her then that Joe Morris had been the first to turn suspicion from her to the floorwalker himself. On the day that he had consulted with Mr. Beadle he had told the latter that he had been shadowing Mr. Shomberg off and on for some time, and only the previous night his efforts had been successful.

It seems he had followed the floorwalker to an obscure millinery shop in a different quarter of the city and there had seen him dispose of goods that were the property of the Lossar-Martin store—at least, so Joe supposed.

He had assumed, said Mr. Beadle, that this information would be greatly valued by Lossar-Martin, and in that assumption he had been correct. A store detective had been set to watch every movement of Shomberg, and this time had caught him in the act.

"But you can thank this Mr. Morris of yours for setting us upon the right track," Mr. Beadle finished, as he held out a hand to Rose. "If I did not know he was pleasantly and profitably employed elsewhere, we would offer him a position in this store as a detective.

"And now, my dear young lady," and he fairly beamed upon Rose, "we wish to apologize for our one-time stupidity in suspecting you and assure you that you may stay with Lossar-Martin as long as you wish."

Rose went out of the office with her head in the clouds.

Joe—Joe Morris had done all this! Mr. Beadle had said that she was to thank him! Would she? Just wait till she saw him!

CHAPTER XXIV

Margy Is Forgiven

Rose had not long to wait.

Leaving the store that evening, she fairly ran into the arms of her deliverer, who was waiting for her outside the employees' entrance.

"Oh, hello, if this isn't our detective himself!" she greeted him gayly, but Joe saw as he took her arm and she glanced up at him that there were tears glistening on her long lashes.

"Joe—Joe, you are such a trump!" she added, huskily. "You don't know what you have saved me from to-day!"

"Why, has anything happened?" cried Joe, with sudden ferocity. "If that Shomberg guy is bothering you again—"

Rose laughed a little hysterically.

"I don't think he will ever bother me after to-day," she told him, and thereupon launched into the story of the day's happenings, told it hastily, with catches of her breath and gaps in between that Joe must fill out for himself.

But he got the general idea and chuckled

with glee at thought of Herbert Shomberg, the lordly and overbearing, being lead away by the head detective.

Rose laughed too, but shakily, and Joe's eyes softened with an understanding of her part in the drama.

"Poor little kid," he said softly. "Must have been pretty hard on you."

"Oh, I don't care." Rose flung up her head with a gallant laugh. "It's all right now—thanks to you, Joe."

Joe blushed with embarrassment, though he liked the way she said "Joe."

"What bothers me," he said thoughtfully, "is how that plume found its way into your locker. Of course, he planted it there himself, but he must be a pretty slick crook to be able to get away with that sort of thing."

"Probably he didn't get away with it," Rose pointed out. "I shouldn't wonder if one of the detectives saw him do it, and that gave him the clew."

Joe went with her all the way to her apartment but, in spite of her invitation, refused to go in.

"I am going to ask you to do something for me though," he said. Rose looked at him inquiringly. "Let me come up to-morrow night?"

"Will I!" cried Rose. "That's a pretty little thing to ask in return for what you have done for me, Joe Morris. Good-bye till to-morrow, Mr. Detective. And—and thank you, Joe!''

Joe did not reply in words, but Rose was still thinking of the way he had looked at her when she reached the door of her own apartment and opened it with her key. She was about to call exuberantly to the girls, eager to tell them of her exciting day, when she paused uncertainly.

She heard a strange voice in the living room—a woman's voice. They had company. It, the company, she reflected, must be unexpected, since Helen had not mentioned expecting any one that morning.

She tiptoed into her room, took off her hat and brushed her shining hair carefully. She saw that her eyes were blazing with excitement and that her cheeks were hotly flushed.

''I wonder who the company is,'' she thought, as she slowly made her way through the hall toward the voices. ''Sounds sort of funny, anyway—short and snappy. Poor Helen, I reckon she won't have enough dinner to go around. We probably have just three chops, and she will give the visitor hers.

This reflection brought her to the door of the living room and she peeped within. What she saw there was so amazing that she completely forgot her manners and stood in the doorway, staring.

There was a little old lady on the couch, a funny-looking little old lady all dressed in stiff black silk with an eccentric black hat with a willow plume atop her gray hair.

She had an arm about Margy and was looking severely from her to Helen and back again. If it had not been for Margy's flushed and happy face and Helen's look of contentment Rose would have guessed that the interview had been an unpleasant one. The little old lady certainly looked cross enough.

It was the bright eyes of the latter who first discovered Rose, standing uncertainly in the doorway.

"Come in, come in!" she cried imperatively. "What an extremely lovely child you are. Over to the light—so. Quite—to be sure."

Utterly bewildered, Rose looked for help to her two sisters. It was Margy who came to the rescue.

"This is Miss Pepper, Rose dear," she said, adding with a happy little laugh: "She has decided to forgive me!"

"Nonsense—utter nonsense," retorted this surprising old person. "How could forgive when nothing to forgive? Ridiculous!"

"It's lovely of you to say so," returned Margy. "You make me very happy when you say that."

"Selfish old person!" exclaimed Miss Pepper, in her disjointed manner. "Please myself—always. Missed you, my dear,'' and she patted Margy's hand with an unusual demonstration of affection. ''Couldn't get along without you. Ridiculous, but true! Must go now,'' she cried, rising with the abruptness that characterized all her actions. ''Come to me, my dear, when feel able. Send doctor's bill to me. All my fault—everything!''

Margy went with her, all the way down the three flights of steps and out to the curb where her handsome limousine was waiting for her. The girl tried to speak as Miss Pepper got into the car and nodded good-bye, but she could not. In silence she watched the big car disappear around the corner, then turned swiftly toward the house.

A few moments later she shut the door of the little apartment and stood with her back against it, looking at the girls with brimming eyes. She took a step toward Helen, tried to laugh, and sobbed instead and collapsed in a big chair, her head in her arms.

That seemed to be the signal, for as Helen and Rose clung to Margy they began to cry too and cried until it struck them all how ridiculous it was to cry for happiness, and then they all began to laugh.

''It seems like a fairy story,'' said Margy, wiping her eyes and smiling unsteadily. ''With me as Cinderella—''

''Miss Pepper seems awfully fond of you,

Marg,'' said Rose, after a moment of happy musing. "If you did but know it, you are a very lucky girl.''

"I think so too,'' admitted Margy. "After to-day.''

It was at that moment that Rose realized she had forgotten all about her own story, and she immediately launched into it, while her sisters listened, astonished and incredulous.

"Why, that Shomberg must be an ogre!'' cried Margy, finally, unable to contain her indignation.

"He is!'' agreed Rose, adding with a chuckle: "But it's all right, as long as I had a fairy prince.''

"And who is he?'' asked Margy, with a look of feigned severity.

Rose opened wide eyes at her.

"Why, don't you know?'' she asked. "His name is Joe Morris, of course!''

CHAPTER XXV

The Check

"I tell you what let's do!"

It was the day after the exciting events at the Lossar-Martin store and Margy's reinstatement in the employ of Miss Pepper. The three girls were having dinner in the small but cheerful dining room with Joe Morris, "the great amateur detective," as their guest.

It had been a merry meal, for the girls had felt like celebrating their good fortune and were accordingly in the highest of spirits. So now, at Rose's exclamation, the three others looked at her expectantly.

"Wouldn't it be great to have a real celebration?" asked the youngest sister as she leaned across the table, cheeks flushed, eyes sparkling.

"If it doesn't cost too much," interjected Helen cautiously. "We aren't millionaires yet, you know."

"Oh, money, money—always money!" Rose tossed her pretty head and pouted adorably. "I wish we could forget it for awhile."

heavy, the heat intense, but she was aware of neither.

Only at the entrance of the apartment was she reminded of a similar occasion when a pleasant gray-eyed young man had kindly carried her work up to her door for her.

Hugh Draper! She would see him to-morrow night, the night of the party. She wondered a little absently why this fact should fill her with happiness.

The evening of the great affair had come. The tiny apartment was shiningly in order and the table in the dining room looked beautiful with its pretty favors and place cards and the huge, three-tier layer cake in the center. Even before the arrival of the guests there was that indefinable atmosphere of festivity that is the inevitable accompaniment of an affair of that sort.

The girls had treated themselves to a new party dress apiece, bought at a special sale. Margy's was a filmy little affair of silver and blue that set off to perfection her brunette coloring. Rose, in pink, exactly matched her name, and Helen was lovely in a soft corn color.

They met in the living room to exchange compliments and excitedly await the coming of their guests.

Birdie North was the first to arrive, and her

coming seemed a signal for the arrival of all the rest. They came in twos and threes and singley until the tiny apartment seemed overflowing with chatter and laughter and youthful exuberance.

Hugh Draper was the last to arrive, but when he did get there he entered into the fun with the best of them. He was really remarkably good looking, and became a marked favorite with the girls almost at the start.

Rose, watching the young lawyer, noticed that his eyes strayed often in Helen's direction and thought generously that she did not blame him. Helen had never looked as lovely as she did to-night.

Some one else seemed to agree with her enthusiastically on that point. Roy Reynolds was making himself as charming to the girl in the corn-color frock as he knew how, and it was well nigh impossible for any one else to get near her.

Any one but Hugh Draper might have given up the attempt altogether. But he was a determined young man, and, besides, he had something to say to Helen that he was determined she should hear. So he watched his chance, and when she slipped out to the kitchen to look after the refreshments he quietly followed her.

"May I come in?" he asked from the kitchen

doorway, and Helen flushed a startled pink as she turned toward him.

"Of course," she answered, recovering and motioning toward an unoccupied chair. "If you don't mind watching me work—"

"Perhaps I can help," he suggested, hopefully, but Helen laughed at him cruelly.

"If you can you are the first man I ever saw who could," she replied, and then, relenting at his injured expression, handed him a plate piled high with cheese and nut sandwiches.

He came back munching one—a sandwich, that is, not a plate!—and Helen smiled.

"You see," she cried, with a helpless gesture, "instead of helping me, you help yourself. Do you think that is nice?"

"Maybe not; but I have something here in my pocket for you that I hope you will think very nice," returned the young man, and the girl, struck by his significant tone, stood still, staring at him.

"What do you mean?" she asked, bewildered.

For answer Hugh Draper delved into his pocket and brought forth a slip of paper which he held toward her invitingly.

"It's yours," he assured her, adding with a chuckle: "Now say I'm not nice, if you dare."

"Why, it's a check!" Helen was regarding the slip of paper incredulously. A check made out to me for—good gracious, what a lot

of money! Why," looking at him helplessly,
"it can't be for me."

"But it is," he assured her quickly. "The
construction company that shattered your ceiling and ruined your work gave me power to
settle with you rather than take the case to the
courts. A thing like that would probably delay their building, and they are willing to pay,
and pay well, to be let alone. Of course, if you
don't think that's enough—"

"Enough!" breathed Helen, still wandering in a delightful daze of incredulity. "Why,
it is more—far more—than I dared dream of!
Mr. Draper, I—don't know how I can thank
you—"

"Well, I declare! are you two going to hold
up this party all night?"

Rose poked her pretty head in at the doorway and over her shoulder could be seen the
cheerfully grinning face of Joe Morris.

Under cover of the general stampede for refreshments, Helen slipped away unnoticed to
her room, where she deposited the precious
check in a safe corner of her bureau drawer.

When she returned to the dining room she
found both Roy Reynolds and the young lawyer
waiting for her, but this time it was Hugh
Draper who won!

It was not till after the last reluctant guest
had departed that Helen told her sisters of the
check.

They retired to the larger of the two bedrooms, and, after carefully hanging up their
party frocks, Margy and Rose launched into a
sleepy but joyful discussion of their wonderful party. But they forgot all about the party
for the moment when Helen brought forth the
check from the construction company and told
how Hugh Draper had given it to her.

"I always said that man was a perfect
prince!" exclaimed Rose, as she handled the
slip of paper. "Goodness, Nell, they can
knock our old ceiling down every night if they
want to!"

"It is wonderful, Helen dear!" cried Margy,
softly, as she drew her sister down on the bed
beside her. "Now you can go on with your
art studies and—everything."

"I believe I can," murmured Helen, her eyes
luminous. "Oh, girls, it begins to look as if—
as if all our troubles were over at last. What
a wonderful old world it is!"

"You said it!" cried Rose and, shaking her
golden curls, dived headfirst into bed. "I
wouldn't change places with a queen, just
now!"

But as life is as full of troubles and per-
plexities as it is of sunshine, the three Blythe
girls were destined to meet their share of ad-
versity in the stirring days to come. How they
met and solved these problems, remaining
brave and fun-loving and unspoiled through-

out, will be told in the next volume of this
series, entitled, "The Blythe Girls: Margy's
Queer Inheritance; or, The Worth of a Name."

But it did seem that, for the time being, at
least, Fate had decided to smile upon the
Blythe sisters and upon all their friends in
the bargain.

Suspicion having been lifted from her by the
arrest of Mr. Shomberg, at the store Rose became a general favorite. Even Miss O'Brien,
shaken in her rule by the defection of the floorwalker, seemed less dictatorial and domineering than of old.

Relieved of the load of anxiety that she had
been forced to carry for so long, Rose put her
heart into her work and succeeded so well that,
one fine morning, Mr. Beadle called her into
his office.

"Your work has improved so much, Miss
Blythe," he said, regarding her benevolently
over his spectacles, "that we have decided to
raise your salary. From the first of the month,
it will be eighteen instead of the usual fifteen
a week."

Rose flushed with pride but the next moment
her face darkened. She turned impulsively to
the smiling assistant manager.

"Oh, Mr. Beadle, I do thank you. But—I
really don't deserve a raise nearly as much as
Miss North does. Truly I don't!"

The man in the swivel chair looked astonished and rubbed his forehead thoughtfully.

"Miss North?" he repeated gropingly. "I
don't believe I remember—"

"Of course you don't—and that's because
she never makes a fuss about the things she
does!" And thereupon Rose told the interested and attentive Mr. Beadle what a wonderful person Birdie North was, how patient and
untiring. She told him about Mrs. North too,
and then stopped suddenly, alarmed at her out-
burst, fearing she had said too much. But Mr.
Beadle's eyes were strangely soft as he said
gently:

"Then you really think this increase in
salary should go to Miss North, instead of
yourself?"

"Oh, yes," said Rose eagerly. "I do!"

The man in the swivel chair studied her a
moment, then smiled.

"Since Miss North is so valuable to the firm
of Lossar-Martin, I see no reason why she
should not be rewarded, too," he said. "Her
salary will also be increased, beginning the
first of the month. You may tell her so, if you
like!"

"Rose, I can't believe it's true. You aren't
joking, are you? You couldn't be so cruel?
Think, just think, what it will mean to
mother!"

"Don't you suppose I haven't?" asked Rose, blinking back the tears of joy that would fill her eyes. "She will be glad, won't she?"

"Glad!" repeated Birdie North, her thin, tired little face bright with a new hope. "Oh, Posie, you don't know the difference it makes —there's a florist—wait a minute, I'll be right back—"

"What are you going to do?" asked Rose as the girl darted toward the shop.

"Buy some roses, of course! As many as I can get for a dollar. And don't you try to stop me, either!"

Rose laughed shakily as she slowly followed her friend.

"What a good old world it is!" she murmured. "What a good old world!"

THE END